Cosmic Heat

AN ALIEN BURLESQUE ROMANCE

GALACTIC GEMS SERIES
BOOK THREE

CLIO EVANS

Copyright © 2024 Clio Evans

Cover Illustration by Kira Night

Character art illustrated by @jemlin_c

Edited by @sarahinwanderland

All rights reserved. No part of this book may be reproduced or used in any manner without the prior written permission of the copyright owner, except for the use of brief quotations in a book review.

No part of this book was written with Artificial Intelligence. I support human creativity and will never use generative AI.

*For every nonbinary star.
Don't ever let anyone steal your light.*

Welcome to the Show...

Prepare to be seduced, horny, and swooning! Here you will find the following:

Use of drugs for sex, flogging, restraints, heats, tentacle cocks, light BDSM dynamics, switch scenes, going into heat, attempted murder, stabbing (not in a fun way), kidnapping, and more.

xoxo THE Madam Moonie

Author's Note: One of the main character's pronouns are **xe, xem, xyr**. These are not typos.

Madam Moonie

THE CRYSTAL OASIS stretched out before me as I leaned over the wooden balcony, letting the warmth of the sun keep my temper from burning everyone around me. My room was at the base of one of the enormous trees that stretched towards the planet Arbor's sky, one of six within the Augelite Galaxy. Below, there were pools of luminescent blue, steam curling up from their serenity, all surrounded by glittering crystals that grew naturally.

As lovely as the Hörne Forest was, the transportation system was a headache. All of our equipment and bags had arrived late. Some of the equipment had arrived damaged. The first person I'd spoken to initially about it all had blown up on me and our conversation had ended in an absurd fight. Eventually, I'd gotten a hold of the manager, but we'd gone back and forth all morning, because they owed us money for damages. They insisted it was out of their control and that humans were just uptight and demanding.

We had a meeting scheduled for this evening, and I'd decided I would invite them to our show. Woo them some. Get them to see that they should, of course, pay us for damages because we were wonderful and stunning creatures worthy of a refund.

I drummed my nails, breathing in and releasing it. Deep breaths. Yoga breaths. Calming energy. Even if I wanted to breathe fire like a gorgeous glittering dragon on anyone that perceived me at the moment, I could not. Not only for the sake of the Galactic Gems, but I had my reputation to uphold.

A soft knock at the door had me turning. "Come in," I called.

Lady Luun, who we all called Lady, poked her head through the door. "I come bearing gifts," she said.

I snorted. "You know I'd never bite you."

She smirked as she slid in, holding a cup of coffee. The scent nearly made my knees weak.

"You are a goddess," I sighed as she brought it to me.

"Surprisingly, they have coffee on this planet. I didn't think they would. But I think we should be able to get enough here so we don't have to worry about our next galaxy trip."

We'd run out of coffee supplies on the ship, which had led to some very cranky members.

Me. I had been the cranky member.

Lady had long turquoise hair that was currently pulled up into a bun and wore a silk robe that nearly swept the floor as she walked or moved, gorgeous as always. "This place is lovely," she said, her eyes shifting to the view from the balcony. "Did everything get worked out?"

"No," I sighed. "It will be fine, though. We'll start rehearsals tonight and evaluate damages and what we'll have to change. Now that Max is a performer, I need to find another assistant. If you can think of anyone, let me know."

"I'll be on the lookout," she said. "I can't think of anyone better than him, though. To think he was so timid when he started."

"Well, I hired him for a reason. I have good instincts."

I took a sip of coffee, and it soothed my woes. Lady was right about Max, but it was his time to shine. The routine he'd been preparing for was going to be a showstopper. If everything went right, then his debut performance would be talked about through all the galaxies.

His stage name was the Maximalist, and perfect for his style of performing. His costumes and visions were over the top, but he pulled it all together with finesse. There'd been some run-throughs where he'd made rookie mistakes, but he was driven. I was confident in him, as I was in all of my performers.

They were my gems, after all.

I went back out onto the balcony and took a seat in a chair that floated above the ground. Lady leaned against the balcony, her silence a comfort. One thing I'd always appreciated about her was that she never rushed to fill the quiet with words.

"How are you feeling?" I asked.

"I'm good. Antsy. I want to be on stage. Hopefully, my moon lyra wasn't damaged."

"It wasn't, thankfully." She sighed, relieved. That thing cost a fortune. "Our lighting crew won't be happy though."

"The stage here is naturally lit, at least. I think everyone here will prefer that."

I agreed. And the stage was lovely. It was in the center of a vast pool and always gave us stunning promotional material. The challenges were many, though. Any rigging had to be set up manually, as there were not metal structures to secure to. Getting the performers to the stage without it being awkward and without them getting wet was another problem, too.

I sighed and closed my eyes, trying not to stress.

It would work out. It always did.

When I opened my eyes, I didn't see Lady—but a vision instead.

Vines and horns, stars and a flash of orange.

As always, I couldn't exactly see who was in the vision. But I felt the heat of their passion, the fire of their desires so strong that sweat beaded my skin.

"Madam? Madam!"

And so it will be.

My eyes fluttered, and I realized that I'd spilled my coffee. Lady was kneeling in front of me, her brows drawn together in concern.

"Damn it, my coffee," I sighed dramatically.

"I can get you another," she said. "What was that?"

"It was a vision. I don't know about whom. But, I won't be surprised if someone is swept off their feet again."

Lady raised a brow. "Does this always happen?"

"Always? No...But recently, I've had two visions. Once before Stella met Zin and Toras and once before Raider abducted Mari..."

Lady laughed. "Oh gods. I forgot he did that. The two of them are so happy."

"They are," I said warmly, smiling.

Raider and Mari were on their honeymoon too and would be at the first show as audience members. And then they'd be off doing whatever they wanted. I was proud of her for taking some time off.

And the cowboy had grown on me. Plus, he could fix anything on the ship. And he looked great in chaps and he was useful.

Stella would be gone soon. She and her mates were spending the first three weeks in this galaxy, and then they'd be gone for two months.

"I wonder who's next," Lady murmured.

I raised a brow. But she had a point. If that was a sign...

For a moment, I thought about adding a fated mate's contract clause, but then decided that would be a bad idea.

Still, it made me snort.

"Let me get dressed and then we can go get some coffee and breakfast?"

"Yes," she said. "Should I invite the entire crew?"

"We'll run into them, I'm sure. I need to see how everyone is settling in."

"Well, my room is perfect. I'm sure everyone else feels the same. We're always spoiled on this planet, even with the logistical difficulties."

She had a point.

"Alright, give me five, and I'll be ready," I said.

Meanwhile, I couldn't let go of the wandering thought—who was next?

CHAPTER 1
The Maximalist

MAX

The silence of the crowd was deafening.

I reminded myself that on this planet, crowds weren't as raucous as others. They weren't as loud. The silence wasn't a bad sign. When the performance started, they would clap and cheer.

But for now? I could hear the rustle of the leaves over any idle chatter. My stomach was full of butterflies. My heart wouldn't stop pounding.

I readjusted my grip on the straps that would soon lift me up into the air. I was thankful for the gel I'd used on my hands that soaked up any sweat. That would keep me from having an injury or fall.

My sequined suit glittered like a thousand stars. The cape I wore was sequined and bright blue, mirroring the oasis that stretched around the stage. It created a circle, and beyond that was where the audience sat. I couldn't see their faces, which was good and bad for my nerves.

This performance was part of me now. I'd lost track of how many times I'd practiced, but this was it.

This was my moment.

My debut performance.

"Breathe," Madam said into my earpiece.

It was her last reminder to me. I could hear the pride in her voice, and that made me smile. It made me relax.

I was one of the gems. I was part of the burlesque troupe now, not just as an assistant, but as a performer—something I'd dreamed of for so long. There had been many people along the way who didn't believe in me, but for those who had, they'd kept me going.

They'd cheered me on.

I breathed out. I was ready. I couldn't be more ready.

"Welcome to the Galactic Gems Burlesque show!"

Madam Moonie's voice echoed through the oasis, smooth and boisterous. She tailored her words for every place we visited, reading into the crowd and how they would best respond.

"We are honored to be here on your planet, in the lovely Hörne Forests. Thank you for welcoming us to your home!"

The crowd clapped, which was a good sign.

"Now...please welcome our newest member to the Galactic Gems. An aerialist, a performer, an eclectic rising star—please welcome the Maximalist!"

I tightened my grip on the straps as they lifted slightly and I curled into a ball, barely raised above the ground. My wrist looped into one of the straps, but I gripped both because soon I would use the two for a variety of moves.

My cape ensconced me as the music started, a soft violin rising into the countless leaves that crowned the venue. I lifted higher and higher, my muscles straining as I stayed in this position. They had become accustomed to the burn.

The music rose and rose, and so did I, until it hit a crescendo.

I burst free, opening up my body like a star. My cape swirled as I began to spin, using the momentum to turn. I reached up, grabbing hold of the second strap and lifting myself, pushing against the straps as I flipped myself upside down.

I heard their claps and cheers. But I did my best to ignore that, focusing on the swell of the music as I moved my body. It thrummed in my veins, every musical note ingrained into me. I wrapped my leg around one strap, freeing a hand so the first piece of clothing could come off.

This was burlesque.

I grinned. They cheered as my cape fluttered to the floor, leaving me in my suit. I unhooked my leg and then slipped my ankle through the loop, moving up so I could do the same to the other. I split my legs in the air, a horizontal line.

I grabbed on to the bow around my neck and gave it a sensuous tug, enjoying their response. I pulled it loose and let it fall to the stage.

I undid the first button of my jacket. My muscles quivered as I held this position, each one of them engaged. I slowly undid the next button and the next, using the movement to engage with the crowd. Finally, the last button came free, and I slid the jacket free, letting it fall down.

Another piece for the stage.

They cheered, their voices rising with the music.

I'd never felt more alive. The energy was addictive, and I felt all of my worries fly away. All the pent up anxiety melted into the moment, into doing what I loved. What I'd always dreamed of.

I went through my performance, giving it everything I could.

Tasseled pasties shook on my nipples as I moved. I was down to them and my suspenders, and then my pants. I flipped upside down again, enjoying their gasps as I grabbed onto the straps, pulling my ankles free and replacing them with my wrists. I rolled up, my shoulder pulled behind me as I hung sideways by one arm.

I pointed my toes, holding as I spun again.

The music thrummed as I reached for my pants. With an easy rip, they came free, the buttons along my legs snapping open, as well as the back. The crowd cheered again, especially now that I was down to pasties, suspenders, and a sparkly pair of very short shorts.

I rolled out of that grip and grabbed onto the straps with both hands, pushing against them and straightening my body back, as if I were doing a plank on the floor...only I was fifteen feet up in the air. I grunted as I held it, living for their applause.

The end was coming soon. I breathed out as I changed into another pose, and then slid my arms through the straps, posing as I rocked back and forth to create momentum. I twirled as the rigging slowly lowered me back towards the floor, spinning faster until my toes met the stage.

I used the momentum and sprinted forward, sliding to my knees. The crowd cheered as I grabbed onto the suspenders, popping them free. I rocked my hips to the beat, sliding across the stage into my last position.

The lights dimmed, the music ending.

"Give it up for the Maximalist!"

The crowd roared.

I was out of breath and covered in sweat, but the euphoric feeling rushing through me was almost better than sex. I huffed as I waited for the cue, seeing a stagehand dashing across for my clothing as I stood. I followed them to the edge of the stage, the dim light hard to see in as I stepped into a small, silent boat.

"You did amazing," they whispered to me.

"Thank you!" I was still breathing hard as I tried to relax.

Crystals that grew on the outer edge of the pool glowed a gentle blue, providing enough light for us. This had to be one of the stranger venues we went to, but it was worth it. A couple of other assistants rowed us to our 'backstage' area.

The clapping didn't die until Madam Moonie's voice came on, talking as the crew rolled everything over for the next performer, Lady Luun. She waved from her little boat as we passed each other.

"Good luck!" I whisper-yelled to her.

Our boat came to the edge, and I stepped out. Stella was waiting there, already dressed for her performance. She wore a stunning crystal corset with a sheer robe that swept around her as she moved. She pulled me into a hard hug.

"You did amazing!"

I sniffled as I started to come down from the high of performing. She leaned back and shook her head.

"If you cry, then I'll cry, and my makeup is perfect," she hissed. "So save those tears for after the show, okay?"

I laughed and blinked them away. "You look flawless and we don't want to ruin that. Are you sure I did okay?"

"Max, you're a natural," she said. "You should be so proud. You've been working your ass off. And now you get to enjoy the rest of the show after you go talk and flirt with the Hörne official."

"The what?" I asked.

Stella made a face and sighed. "Madam Moonie is fighting to get our damages covered, and it ended up going to one of the forest officials. They're not royalty, but they're like a...mayor? I guess? I don't know. Madam wants us all to greet them."

Stella gestured behind her and I peeked around her shoulder.

Standing a few feet away was a *very* tall Arborian who was absolutely breathtaking. They had smooth purple skin and wore long, elaborate blue robes with intricate gold details. A hammered gold collar gleamed around their neck, and earrings dripped from their potted ears. They had long hair that framed their chiseled face. And then there were their horns—a rack that went from dark purple, to pink, to bright orange—reminding me of vibrant branches.

They were stunning.

"Go say hi," Stella whispered. "And try not to drool on them."

I gave her a look, but she didn't hide her smirk as I slipped past her and went towards them. I hesitated as I approached, but as their gaze met mine, I felt drawn towards them, a magnetic field pulling me in.

My head craned back as I looked up at them. "Hi, I'm Max," I said.

Their eyes seemed to darken for a moment, the frosty violet turning deep purple. They blinked and their color returned to normal. "You can call me Moss," they said. "Can I help you?"

Yeah, you could help me.

They immediately scowled as if they'd heard my thought and took a step back, which hurt way more than it should have coming from a stranger. And especially since I hadn't even said anything.

I crossed my arms and cleared my throat. "Enjoying the show?"

"Yes. Humans are very talented, although loud sometimes."

"Arborians are very quiet," I countered.

The corner of their mouth tugged into a smile. "Not always."

I didn't know what to make of that and now felt awkward. I was supposed to be riding the high of my first performance, not fumbling through a conversation with a hot alien.

"I hope you enjoy the rest of the show," I said.

I slipped past them, but I wasn't paying attention to the ground. My foot hooked under a root and I fell forward, but then Moss was there, their broad hands catching me in the blink of an eye.

The moment they touched me, three things happened at once.

One—an electric current ran through my body that made me gasp, and made them gasp too.

Two—my cock hardened as pleasure buzzed through me.

Three—they immediately released me and I fell flat on my face.

"Fuck," I grunted, pushing up. I froze as I registered how painfully obvious it would be if I stood right now. *Oh gods, what am I supposed to do?*

Moss crouched down, covering me with their robes. They let out a low snarl as they hovered over me. "You are trouble," they growled.

"Me?" I hissed. "*What* was that?"

"Shh," they snapped. "Sit up, human."

"Max. My name is Max."

"Max. Please, sit up." The plea in their voice alarmed me.

"I'm..." I trailed off, blushing hard. What the hell was happening?

Instead of waiting for me to move, they scooped me up with ease. Their body felt feverish against mine, radiating waves of energy I swear hadn't been there before. "Dressing room. Do you have a private one? This is a problem. A horrible, horrible problem." They let out a soft string of curses that were too fast for my translator.

"Yes, it's a room at the base of this tree. I don't understand what happened?"

All I'd done was fall flat on my face in front of them.

They were already moving. We earned a few curious glances from stagehands and crew, but everyone was in show mode. I could hear Lady Luun's music and knew Stella was next.

Moss rushed through the carved opening at the base of the tree, their horns gleaming in the amber lighting that shone around us.

"Down on the right," I said.

I should have demanded they put me down. Instead, I held onto their robes as they carried me down the hall to the last door on the right. They kicked open the door and stepped in, shutting it behind.

"What is happening?" I asked.

They set me down, their brows drawing together into a scowl. I stepped back from them, my every defense going up. They paced back and forth, making a series of growls that I couldn't interpret.

"There is something about you that has ruined me," they finally said, casting me an accusatory glance.

"I don't know what you mean. We just met," I said, crossing my arms. I did nothing to hide my cock or how hard it was against my shorts. "And honestly, for this, your company should pay for the damages."

"The damage payment is the least of my concerns," they growled.

"What is your problem?" I growled.

They stepped closer, towering over me, but not in a way that was intimidating. In fact, if anything, it only turned me on more.

"You are my problem," they said. "You've sent me into sporev. Just by touching you."

"I stared at them, holding their slightly panicked gaze.

"I don't know what that means," I whispered.

"You do, given that you appear to be aroused."

"Well, I am," I muttered, my cheeks now burning red hot. "For whatever reason."

"Our pheromones are causing this. You've sent me into sporev, which means my pheromones are now much stronger and... It's like a heat. A sexual frenzy is taking us over as we speak, and there's only one way to satisfy it."

"How?" I asked.

"By bedding you."

CHAPTER 2
Predicaments

MOSS

Propositioning a human to come to my bed had not been on my list of things to do today—or ever. The way my blood burned for him was almost unbearable as I breathed in his scent.

When we touched, something primal within me snapped. It was almost so fierce that it was audible. A moment, a mistake, and now I was cornering a burlesque dancer in his dressing room, begging him to let me mate with him.

I knew this could happen to Arborians. It was a somewhat common occurrence, however, it usually meant that you'd found your mate. A few days of sexual release followed by knowing that you'd probably found the one the universe deemed to belong with you.

But a human...a human wouldn't understand the implications, right? I stared at Max, wondering how the universe could do this to us. And yet, the part of my being that craved him like he was a basic need, a breath of fresh air or a sip of cold water... it was different.

Max made an expression I couldn't quite understand. His lips pressed together, his brows drawing close. He stared and then shook his head.

"The only way to overcome this heat is by having sex with me?"

"Yes," I said. "It will be the same for you. My pheromones have taken yours. Even as a human, your body has already decided that it wants mine. That doesn't mean we have to."

"What happens if we don't?"

Suffering. Months and months of suffering until it waned, but I wouldn't be satisfied for a long time, and neither would Max.

He seemed to read into my silence and sighed. He raked his fingers through his bright orange hair. "Madam Moonie is going to be furious."

Madam Moonie. The leader of the Galactic Gems, who was very protective of her crew. I understood her, because I was the same with my own.

It was a predicament. One that I had not foreseen or even considered might happen. And yet... "I'll pay for the damages to the equipment if you help me solve this heat," I whispered.

Max raised a brow and then crossed his arms. "If we're going to have sex, it doesn't need to be transactional. Either choose to pay for the damages and then we'll take care of our problem or don't."

I winced. I hadn't meant for this to sound that way. I cursed our languages and the translators we each had, not sure how to clarify.

"I didn't mean it that way," I said.

Max stared for a moment longer and then crossed the small room to a bench that was covered in clothing. He slid off his suspenders and then grabbed the edge of his shorts. He pulled them down, revealing another swath of clothing that he also pulled free.

My mouth watered at the sight of his ass. A human's body was not so different from an Arborian's in some ways, but I still found myself studying and appreciating every part of him.

"Are your pronouns he?" I asked.

Max nodded. "Yes. Are yours they and them? Everyone had referred to you as they or them."

"It's a little different, but I found that they or them are easiest for humans."

"Oh. I'll use whatever they are," he said as he dressed.

He pulled on a sleek pair of pants and a billowing shirt with an open V neck, and then a pair of boots. He turned to face me.

"Truly," he said. "What are your pronouns?"

"Xe, xem, xyr."

"Some humans use xe as well," he said. He continued to study me warily. "I'll let others know too, if you'd like. I think you'll find our entire crew won't find it hard to use your correct pronouns."

I breathed out. Perhaps there was more to humans than I realized. Aside from the tourists that graced our planet, I rarely met humans. And the burlesque show tonight was my first one.

I didn't get out of the tree enough, it seemed. Too busy at work and trying to keep everything from falling apart. In fact, the only extracurricular activities I ever took part in were sexual...and now all I could think about was applying my knowledge to the little human in front of me.

Max offered me a genuine smile. I felt myself relax, even if desire and need engulfed my entire body. I was walking on a knife-edge, but I'd suffer the pain for now.

"I'm sorry for being brusque," I mumbled. "And I'm sorry I let you fall. Are you okay?"

Max wrinkled his nose. "I have taken way worse. I'm fine. If we have to deal with this...predicament, we'll need to talk to Madam Moonie first."

"Are you not able to do as you please?" I asked.

"I am, but I don't want to worry my boss. Tonight was my first performance and disappearing after it to sleep with the alien she's trying to get to agree to something isn't an impressive look."

He had a point. First performance. Do I gift him something for such an event? I felt a flood of panic, followed by the two tentacles throbbing beneath my robes.

"The show runs for another twenty minutes and then there is an intermission. We can try to talk to her then, I guess...I don't even know how to phrase it."

"Leave it to me," I said decidedly, straightening my shoulder. "Wait here. I shall return."

I was out of the room before he could argue, flying down the hall of one of our great Hörne trees and out into the open. I could see the performer at the center of the oasis, along with the crowd beyond them that cheered wildly for her performance. Her voice rose up, a smooth, beautiful melody that made me pause.

All the performers were talented. Even if this predicament with Max hadn't happened, I would have felt persuaded to cover costs for the damaged equipment. It didn't help that our transportation system was outdated. There were some council members that were stuck in their old ways and wanted to focus funds onto other projects. Dio, a transportation agent whom Madam had spoken to first, worsened the whole situation. Being new to the field, he did not take her words kindly and escalated the entire situation to me to handle. If Madam

Moonie had talked to me first, everything would have gone smoother. Because now, not only were we going to cover the damages, I had to punish Dio for the way he handled everything.

That was tomorrow's problem, though.

The more the worlds became connected, the more visitors we saw. Eventually, we would have to change things. This planet was no longer just our own.

The song ended, and Madam Moonie's voice rose above the venue again. I slipped through the bustling area, avoiding running into any of the humans. Like Max, most of them were a few hands shorter than me, and I worried about knocking into one by accident.

I saw a Lazulian waiting and approached him and then froze when I saw his floating crown. He turned slightly and raised a brow.

"Yes?"

"I'm looking for Madam Moonie. Are you here for the show?"

"Yes. Stella is my mate. Madam Moonie is over there," he said, pointing towards a group of bustling humans. I could see her now, her eyes focused on the stage.

"Thank you," I said. I studied him for a moment longer, not sure if I was supposed to bow. I wasn't sure about their customs. In our world, royalty would never be seen out without protection.

"You seem worried," he said. "My name is Zin."

"You are royalty," I said.

"I am. Are you concerned?"

"No," I breathed out. I had other problems. "The human has caused a predicament. Well, perhaps it was me. The universe? I have to go."

Zin snorted. "Which human?"

"Max," I said.

He gave me a small smile. "Good luck. They'll steal your heart, these little beautiful beings." His gaze swept out towards the stage as the crowd cheered to the woman that ended her song. "I must go. My other mate is retrieving water and we will meet her when she arrives in this area."

I gave him a curt nod and then went towards Madam Moonie. Her eyes met mine and her gaze was razor sharp. She held up a hand as she tapped a mic, her voice rising again.

"Give it up again for Stella Starz and her out-of-this-world Solar Strip!"

Their cheers thundered through the oasis. I waited patiently as she introduced the next star, someone that went by Milky Maid. As soon as the music started, Madam Moonie moved her mic and gave me a look that could kill.

"I am working," she said. "Do you have an emergency?"

"Yes, actually. I will cover the costs of the damage, but I need your performer named Max for three earth days."

Her lips parted, and then she let out a low, sultry laugh. "I'm sorry—what? You can't just have one of my performers."

"He is my—"

"Madam!"

I was startled as Max appeared next to me. He looked up at me, giving me a pinched expression, and then focused on Madam Moonie. If there was communication in his look to me, I did not know what it meant.

"I will still be at rehearsals," Max said. "I'd like to spend some time with Moss...I just didn't want you to worry about my absence."

She looked at him, then me, then back to him. "Gods damn it," she sighed. She pressed her fingers to her temples, her long nails glittering in the light coming off the crystals that grew around us. "It's happening again. Listen—if the two of you end up mated, married, pregnant—whatever—Max still has to work in my troupe. I can't give him up. He's a star and just now starting his career."

The two of us made a series of sputtering noises at her abruptness, but she held up a hand, silencing us both.

"I don't want to hear it. I don't want to know. Be safe, have fun, show up to rehearsal or I'll skewer your lover...." She gave me a very pointed look that I managed to understand. She trailed off and then smirked at Max. "Arborians are fun in bed. Drink some water so you can walk at rehearsal."

Max's mouth fell open, and then she made a hissing noise.

"Both of you go. I have a job to do. And damn it, Max, we were going to celebrate you tonight."

"You still can," I insisted. "I don't want to interrupt anything. I'll come after."

Madam smirked suggestively. "Good. Go away."

Max surprised me by slipping his hand into mine, or trying to, and tugging me to the side. I grabbed his wrist gently and pressed my palm against his, seeing how much smaller his hand was than mine. And to think that I'd seen him turn himself upside down and in various positions using these hands...his palms were rough in places and I couldn't help but think about how they would feel against my skin.

"Moss," Max whispered hoarsely.

I sucked in a breath, which was a mistake. Max's arousal was apparent in his scent, which reminded me of the sweet *tarax* that bloomed every few years in certain oases. A bright orange flower with a long stamen, that produced a scent so intoxicating, so...

"Get a fucking room," Madam Moonie hissed at us.

Max made a noise and grabbed my wrist with both hands, marching me away from the backstage area. We received curious glances again as he pulled me back to his dressing room, tugging me inside and slamming the door shut.

"Did I do something wrong?" I asked.

"No," he huffed, still pushing me.

I let him guide me to the bench. He grabbed onto the lapels of my robes and gave me a very demanding command.

"Sit."

I narrowed my gaze at him. He didn't realize yet that in the bedroom, I'd be the one commanding him. So I'd let him have this firm tone for now.

I sat on the bench, which put my face at the same height as his.

"The show has about forty minutes left. I still have a curtain call. And then we'll have to pick up everything, and then there will be whatever Madam planned."

"Do you want me to leave?" I whispered.

"No." He swallowed hard, his eyes shifting down my robes. "I can lock the door in here."

I stared at him and he stared at me until his cheeks were practically radiating heat.

"You don't do well with insinuations, do you?" he mumbled.

"It's difficult with our translators," I said.

He nodded. "May I touch you?"

"Yes."

He reached up and cupped my face. "I want you to fuck me before the show ends so I don't die of horniness between now and midnight."

It was my turn to be completely shocked. My tentacles writhed, aching for him, aching to be inside him. Or to have him inside me...

"We don't need to rush," I whispered, although I could feel the heat radiating from my body.

He leaned in closer, his lips almost touching mine. "Do you want me?"

"More than you can possibly imagine," I said.

"Then are you scared?"

His taunt made me growl. "May I touch you?"

"Yes."

The moment he consented, I grabbed his hips and lifted him, seating him directly on my lap with his legs straddling me. He gasped, his eyes widening as I grabbed his wrist and tugged them behind his back, holding them in place with one hand.

"If we were not in a dire emergency, I would spend weeks courting you," I snapped. "Even if I don't understand you all that well yet, I promise I will by the end of our heat. Tell me, what kind of things please you, Max? What makes you want to submit?"

His eyes widened again. "Submit?"

I raised a brow. "You didn't think I would be the one submitting, did you?"

"Maybe I did."

"And now?"

I could feel his cock against me.

"Now, I think it's clear you like to be in control..." He licked his lips. "I enjoy being told what to do. Nicely, of course."

"How much do you know about my kind?" I asked.

"Well, I know your planet is beautiful and that you're all very tall and..."

"And of my genitalia? I know about humans. It's been awhile since I've read up on human anatomy, but I certainly..." I trailed off as I unbuttoned his pants. "...haven't..." I slid my hand in and gripped his cock. "...forgotten."

He moaned, his head falling back. A silent curse left his lips, his hips rocking against me.

I released him and enjoyed the sharp look I received for toying with him.

"Show me," he whispered. "If you'd like..."

I let him stand up and reached around my robes, unlatching part of it so that I could pull the fabrics back. He fell to his knees in front of me as I revealed myself.

Two dark purple tentacles with orange tips, like my horns. Small suckers ran along the bottoms of each one, and between them...

I reached down, pulling the top tentacle up and revealing an opening and a small nub that was similar to a human clit.

"Wow," he whispered.

"Touch me," I murmured. "If you'd like to explore."

The tentacles moved by themselves, writhing as I released the top one, only to be replaced by his hand. Again, just a touch shared between us was enough to make me groan. I gripped the edge of the bench as he explored me.

He gently circled the small nub at the base of the tentacle, and I whimpered.

"Is this like a clit?" he asked.

"Yes," I breathed out.

"And then your...tentacles..."

"Are like cocks. When I orgasm, fluid will leave their tips as well."

Max licked his lips. "And then this opening..."

"Is it similar to a vagina in human terms..."

He let out a soft hum. "Your body is like what humans dream about and then turn into sex toys."

I chuckled as he gripped the upper tentacle, sliding his hand up and down. Pleasure rolled through me, my breaths shortening as I fought the urge to take things further.

I was hanging on by a thread.

"If we start, we won't stop," I rasped. "We should wait until your evening is finished. I can leave if needed."

"You can join us if you want," he murmured. He held my tentacle for a moment longer and then released it carefully, biting his lower lip. "Somehow, we'll wait a few hours."

"And then I hope you don't plan to sleep."

"I certainly don't..."

"I'll bring you to my home," I said. "The Crystal Oasis is nice, but I think the privacy of my space would be beneficial." I pulled my robe around and adjusted my clothing.

He breathed out and smiled up at me. A piece of hair loosened, curling against his warm ochre skin. I reached up, brushing it back gently.

This evening had truly taken a turn for the two of us.

"Can we even be in public together, or will we both just be horny messes?" he teased.

"Horny messes. My tentacles are easier to hide than your own member."

"Member," he teased. He stood up and brushed his hands down his body. "I think we'll live. Let's try to enjoy the rest of the show."

CHAPTER 3
Moon Bridge

MAX

It was torture for both of us.

By the time the show ended, I felt like I had a fever. The stage and backstage were cleared, and everyone gathered around to congratulate me on an amazing first performance. I could feel Moss's presence everywhere, even if xe was standing a few feet away.

Madam Moonie popped a bottle of expensive champagne and poured everyone a bubbling flute.

"As always, the show was a hit. Thank you to all the performers and of course, our crew. I know this venue has its challenges but we have a beautiful few weeks ahead of us. Here's to our success!"

Everyone cheered and clinked glasses. Stella bumped shoulders with me as we both downed ours.

"Are you leaving with the official?" she whispered.

"Is it that obvious?" I whispered back.

"Zin ran into them," she said.

"It's xem," I said. "Xe, xem, xyr."

"Oh! Thank you," she said. "Good to know. Zin said xe was *flustered*. And no offense, but you look like a hot mess right now."

"I'm always a hot mess. Now that everything is finished, I'm going to make my stage left." I gave her a hug and kissed her cheek, spotting Toras and Zin over her shoulder. "I think your mates are waiting for you too."

"They are," she snickered. "Have fun, be safe."

With our quick goodbye, I looked up, searching for Moss. Xe waited patiently near the water's edge. I made my way to xem and craned my head back, meeting xyr gaze. "I'm ready. I need to grab my bag—"

Xe lifted it with a slight smile. "Done."

"Then let's go to my room, drop it off, and I'll pack some other items to wear."

"You won't need clothing."

I wasn't sure xe meant xyr words to sound so sexual, but we certainly both felt it.

"How about you go and I'll meet you? We will take a different form of travel to get to my place..."

I wasn't sure exactly what xe meant, but I wasn't in the right mind to ask. The two of us made our way around the edge of the oasis to one of the massive trees that towered above us like an enormous cathedral, complete in its intricate beauty. The suns had long set, the sky a deep glimmering blue that shone with countless stars and two moons. The crystals that grew cast enough light that we could see.

We went through an entryway, and then up a set of spiraling stairs that led to the third floor. I was practically running to my room, the adrenaline pumping through me, fresh and potent. I already had the high from the performance, but what was happening with Moss and I was something entirely different.

I unlocked the door and we both stepped in. Moss ducked xyr head carefully, making sure xe didn't knock xyr horns on the doorway. I became painfully aware of how messy my space was. The decoration of the room was very natural and contrasted greatly with the random glitter, costume pieces, sequins, and boots that scattered everywhere.

"Ignore the mess," I mumbled, snatching the bag from xem.

Xe waited patiently as I darted around the room, dumping everything out of my bag on the bed, and then stuffing other clothing that was presumably clean into it. I went to the bathroom and grabbed a small cosmetics bag, catching a glimpse of myself in the mirror.

I was really about to take off with an alien because we were both in heat and the only solution was to fuck.

Breathe. It's not like this is the craziest thing you've ever done.

There were many times I'd make reckless decisions. And if this was truly a bad idea, Madam Moonie or Stella would have said something...

I felt the edge of the sexual delirium begging both of us to give in. It was like a carnal pressure building within.

And I needed the release.

Fuck.

I gathered the rest of my things and left the bathroom, shoving them into my bag. This would be a one night stand... three night stand? However long, and then I'd probably not see xem much. We were here for six weeks, but...

I shoved those thoughts away. I was getting way ahead of myself.

When I turned, Moss was right there. Xe caught my shoulders gently, steadying me.

"You are like a little bee buzzing around frantically right now," Moss said softly. "I promise I won't bite you unless you ask."

I went still, trying to keep my heart from bursting out of my chest. I held xyr gaze, letting it calm me. "It's been awhile since I've done something like this."

"For me, too," Moss said. "Even with the heat...if you decide to leave, you can. I'm not going to trap you or keep you against your will."

"Okay," I said, relaxing.

Xe smiled and reached for my bag, picking it up for me. "Come with me. We're taking the Arborian way of travel, which humans don't see much of. My home is about half an hour from here."

"Excellent," I said. "I'm ready."

I hadn't been sure of what to expect, but Moss pulling me onto xyr back like a backpack and telling me to hold on while they scaled a tree in the dark was not it.

Humans could not move like this. I held onto xem for dear life as xe seemed to step on invisible steps, moving with an ease that amazed and terrified me. The crystals below soon became nothing more than a soft glow, and the moons above gave us more light than anything else.

Some of the trees had rooms, and within were the soft amber glow of artificial light. The further we climbed, the sooner they disappeared as well.

It wasn't until we were at the top of this tree that xe slowed, walking on one of the massive branches. It was wide enough to hold an solarcar. I hadn't realized how large the leaves were, either. The wind picked up, swirling Moss's robes as xe continued.

I realized that the tips of xyr horns glowed soft orange flares in the darkness.

The view of this world from up here was breathtaking, even at night. Maybe more so at night. I looked up, seeing the crowns of every tree in the forest that stretched as far as I could see, disappearing in the distance.

"Your eyes can not perceive all of the colors mine can, especially at night," Moss said. "There is a bridge between the trees that will appear invisible. Don't fret."

Xe said that right as xe stepped into the open air. I let out a short scream, but instead of us tumbling down to the iridescent pools below, Moss carried us with ease over the invisible path.

"I can feel your heart racing against my back," xe chuckled.

"Fuck off," I mumbled playfully.

I found the courage to look down again and wished that I could see through Moss's eyes. I wanted to know the colors I couldn't see, to observe the beauty of xyr planet as xe did.

Two of the moons were close together while the third seemed to orbit on the other side of the sky, much smaller but still beautiful. Moss stepped onto another wide branch of a new tree and continued on the trek.

"I'm sorry that you have to carry me," I said.

"I like carrying you. It would have taken us much longer to get to my home otherwise. As you've seen, our transportation methods are a little outdated, but...we don't want to pollute our planet or over build."

"I can see why," I said.

"The transportation situation wouldn't have been so bad, but your Madam Moonie happened to talk to one of my new people who is known to be obstinate."

"Madam is very commanding in her presence. Anyone who opposes her is typically crushed."

Moss chuckled. "I can see that. She is very strong."

"I think she dated an Arborian once..."

"Perhaps. Many of us have moved to other planets and galaxies. And as we mate with others, they come here too."

I thought about this being my home for a moment. I was a flash of glitter and gold in a world of wood and leaves. And there was nothing wrong with that, but would I fit in?

Why am I thinking about this?

The wind picked up again, but this time, it carried a soft tune. I raised my head, looking out and wondering where the sound came from. It sounded like an ocarina.

"When the wind traverses through certain trees, it creates a song," Moss said softly. "Many of us believe it is the melody of those long gone comforting us or encouraging us."

The melody was warm and gentle. When I breathed again, I felt myself relax even further.

Moss went from tree to tree. Eventually we passed other Arborians too, and I expected for them to look at me strangely, but they didn't.

"We're almost there," xe said softly.

The trees were a little different in this area, I realized. They were more spread out and even larger than the ones around the Crystal Oasis. There were more windows and openings too, and I could occasionally see into those simply living their lives.

"Do you stay up very late?" I asked.

"We sleep on a three Earth-day cycle," xe answered. "Now the trick is to sync your cycles in your friend groups." Xe snickered and I smiled.

Moss climbed further up until xe stopped at a doorway with a door that was barely discernible from the tree itself. Xe pressed xyr palm to the rough bark and it glowed, the door sliding open. Xe stepped inside and let me down.

The door slid closed behind us, blending in with the walls of the tree. The lights came on automatically, blooming through xyr home.

"Wow," I whispered, looking around.

Moss's home was the perfect blend of natural modernity. It was very open, but warm. There was a living area with a comfortable looking hammock and wooden stools with cushions. A kitchen led to a balcony with transparent doors that looked out to the rest of the forest.

"There are two bedrooms and a bathroom."

"This is beautiful," I said.

My home was on the ship. A tiny room of metal, pipes, and costumes. I loved it because it was mine and I'd earned my spot on the Galactic Gems, but I appreciated this home as well.

"Are you hungry?" Moss asked. "I can cook. Or are you sleepy? Do you need a shower? Or water?"

I slid my arms around xem with a snort, pressing my face against xyr chest. Moss let out a soft hum and rested xyr chin on the top of my head.

I wasn't sure where the intimacy was coming from, but I still held onto xem, basking in xyr presence and drinking it in.

"How large is your shower?" I asked.

"It's difficult to explain. I'll show you."

Moss lifted me and carried me princess style down a hall and to a room that made my mouth drop.

"How are there hot springs in the middle of a tree?" I asked.

Steam curled up from a pool at the center, which had the same glowing water as the oasis'. The ceiling was covered in crystals.

Moss smiled. "You're making me feel quite proud of our little world."

"I want to see your bedroom," I said.

Xe turned and carried me to another room. The lights came on, a soft amber glow around a massive round bed in the center. I looked up and realized that branches grew through the ceiling, leaves blooming here and there.

"When the sun is up, it casts light in here," Moss said. "It's my favorite room."

"I can see why," I whispered.

Moss stood still for a moment and then carried me to the bed, settling me down on the edge. I grabbed xyr robe and tugged xem forward on top of me. Xe planted xyr hands to either side of me, xyr lips hovering above mine.

"That was absolute torture," I rasped. "We should have fucked in the dressing room."

"We wouldn't have stopped," Moss teased gently. "You'll grow tired of me, I'm sure."

I wasn't so sure. What had started out as one of the most awkward encounters of my life had turned into something that was hot and new and alluring.

A stark purple line ran from xyr bottom lip and down xyr chin, and xyr neck, disappearing behind xyr hammered gold necklace. I leaned forward and traced xyr bottom lip with the tip of my tongue. When Moss sucked in a breath, I realized that xe had sharp canines, reminding me of a vampire.

"Max," xe whispered.

"Touch me," I rasped. "Take me."

All of the pent up passion caught fire. Moss grabbed the front of my shirt and tore it free, xyr massive palms running over my chest as our lips met.

The taste of xem alone made my cock harden. I thrust my hips up, grinding against xyr body. I grabbed the robes and tugged at them, only for Moss to lean back and reach into them, unlatching the fabrics.

They slid down, pooling at the floor around xyr feet.

"*Holy fuck*," I mumbled.

I loved Moss's robes. However, they hid all of xyr muscles and strength of xyr body, which I was now drooling over. My cock strained against my pants as Moss tilted xyr head, xyr horns beautiful and drawing my gaze before I refocused on xyr tentacle cocks.

Moss reached for my pants and undid them with ease. Xe pulled them off, followed by the tight boxers I wore, piling the last of my clothing on the floor with xyrs.

"I'm going to devour you," xe murmured.

"Please," I huffed. "I need to feel you. I need to touch you."

Moss leaned down and kissed me, gently at first, and then it turned into a raging heat, one that would surely burn us both.

CHAPTER 4
Pollinai

MOSS

Every part of my body yearned for Max. It was something that went beyond words, deeper than my thoughts could convey.

Our tongues met in a tangle as we kissed and I ran my hands down his body, admiring the feel of his muscles beneath my palms. My tentacle cocks were already self lubricating, readying to be inside of my *pollinai*.

My lover.

Max reached down and grasped one of my tentacles, letting out a surprised moan. I broke our kiss with a pant, looking down between us.

"They are ready for you," I whispered. "To be inside of you." *To breed you.*

I didn't say that even if I thought it. My instincts became almost unbearable, everything within me urging me to be inside Max. I moaned, almost painfully.

"We still need lube," Max said quickly. "My bag has some."

"*Sario*," I mumbled.

"What does that mean?" he asked.

I chuckled as I released him. "It means...fuck? Fuck. I'll be back."

"I'll be here," he said with a sly smirk. He slid his hand down to his cock as I backed out of the room, giving it a few strokes.

I rushed out of the room and found Max's bag. I unzipped it and reached in, feeling around for a bottle until I found it.

"Thank you," I whispered, sending up a silent prayer to whomever might listen.

My tentacles writhed as I rushed back to my room. As I entered, I froze, my lips parting in surprise.

Max was on all fours, his ass facing me. He looked over his shoulder and raised a brow.

I let out a low, possessive growl and rushed to him. I opened the bottle of lube and poured a generous amount on the tips of my fingers, running it over his hole. I gently eased a fingertip inside of him, enjoying the way he gasped.

"Fuck," he moaned.

I kept teasing him, trying to keep myself from going too fast. I didn't want to hurt him. My tentacles were somewhat flexible at first, but they would stiffen within him when I came.

"I'm going to breed this little hole," I whispered.

Max cast me a lustful glance. "Please. I want you to."

"I know you do," I sighed happily.

I eased another finger inside of him, working the two of them together until he was stretched enough to take one tentacle. Already, his body was starting to change, reacting to my pheromones and readying for me.

The frenzy was just starting between us.

I grabbed hold of his hips and rose up behind him, pressing the tip of a tentacle against him. His shoulders tensed for a moment as he braced himself, but then a ripple of pleasure passed through both of us.

I gently pushed forward. It writhed within him, moving back and forth of its own accord, the suction cups tugging with him.

"Oh fuck," he gasped.

He pushed his hips back, sinking my cock deep within him. He held still for a moment, even as I kept moving with him.

My bottom tentacle curled around his balls gently, tugging them.

"Oh gods," he cried out.

His voice echoed through my home as I started to move my hips, dragging myself in and out of him. I growled, desperate to fill him with my seed, to give him everything over and over. My lower tentacle continued to milk him, reminding me that soon, I'd have him inside of me too.

The pleasure that shot through me was immense. I could feel a connection in our bodies, deep and satisfying. I wanted to know more. I *needed* to feel him.

Our skin slapped together and joined the chorus of our grunts and groans. I moaned and felt liquid dripping from the tip and suckers. It lubricated him with my copious amounts of precum.

"Harder," he whimpered. "Fuck, your cock is so hot inside of me."

I leaned forward over his body and wrapped my arms around his waist, pulling him back as I stood up. He gasped as I held him in place, slipping my arms beneath his thighs as I continued to fuck him, taking him deeper and deeper, all while squeezing his balls.

I wanted to see him like this.

There was a mirror in the corner of the room. I kept moving as I carried him to it, watching our bodies in the reflection becoming one. His expression was glorious, especially the way his eyes widened when he saw the mirror.

"Fuck!"

Streaks of milky cum shot from his cock, dripping back down his shaft.

I didn't slow. I couldn't. Not yet, not when I was so close to the edge of filling him for the first time. Of marking him as mine. I wanted to bury my seed so deep inside of him, to brand his insides as my *pollinai*.

"Mine," I growled, holding his gaze as my second tentacle unwrapped from his balls, the tip moving towards his hole.

I drew them out and then they came together. With a hard thrust, I pushed both of them inside of him.

His scream of pleasure rang around me. I stilled, holding him as we both panted.

"Don't stop," he begged. "Please don't stop."

The scent of his cum egged me on. His scent was so potent to me, it was like a drug. I pumped into him, my eyes shutting as my body took over.

Mine. He's mine.

Those words struck me with every thrust.

"Max," I moaned.

With a final thrust, my control snapped. I gasped as pleasure rolled through me and I came, my seed bursting within him. I moaned, letting the euphoric rush come over me. The flames of our heat were contained, but only for now.

He was panting as I stepped closer to the mirror, watching as a line of his cum dripped down his cock to his balls.

"There's so much inside me," he rasped. "It feels…"

He trailed off, his head shaking as he whimpered again.

"What's happening to me?"

"My seed is making everything more intense," I whispered. "Now that it's inside of you every orgasm will be so much more pleasurable. Your stamina will be increased and you shouldn't feel any pain, even if we were to fuck for hours."

"Wow," he mumbled. "A lot of benefits."

There were. I slowly eased out of him, watching in satisfaction as my cum dripped from him, pooling at my feet. My tentacles came free, slick and still pulsating.

"That was incredible," he whispered.

We were nowhere near done. I carried him back to the bed and climbed onto it, laying back and moving him. He squeaked as I brought his thighs around my face, pulling his ass to my mouth.

"Moss—*fuck!*"

I thrust my tongue inside of him as he planted his hands on my lower stomach. I tasted myself inside of him, moaning against his body as he rode my face.

He leaned forward, sliding his hand around the top tentacle. He pulled it back, and I could feel his gaze on my opening.

My tongue thrust deeper, my fingertips digging into his hips. I forced myself to slow, to take everything in instead of losing control. But he was making it difficult, especially as he began to explore me. He pressed the tip of his tongue against my sensitive little nub, and I cried out, my voice muffled against him.

Pleasure rushed through me, pulsing as his tongue circled my clit. I growled, lifting him for just a moment to catch my breath. I panted as he continued, his tongue dipping inside of me.

Sario. For a moment, I felt like I was dying and living at the same time, the pleasure so overwhelming that I stopped breathing. My eyes squeezed shut as he pleased me, setting every nerve ending on fire.

I came again, my seed bursting from my cocks. He grabbed

onto the base of both tentacles, licking up every drop of my cum before returning to me slick opening.

"I want to fuck you," he rasped.

I wanted him to as well. "You can," I moaned.

He slid off my body, turned around, and looked up at me. "Lube?"

I shook my head. "We don't need it. I am in heat and slick. I want your cock inside of me, Max."

He blew out a breath, his body gleaming with sweat. He threw his leg over my thighs, straddling me as he looked down at my body. The way his brown eyes burned with need made me writhe.

"How many times can you come?" he whispered.

"It's endless," I moaned. I arched beneath him, the desperation crawling through me like a thousand ants. "The fever has taken me. I *need* you to fuck me."

He let out a little groan and leaned down, planting a hand on the bed beside my ribs. He lined up the head of his cock with my opening and gasped as the lower tentacle wrapped around his balls again.

"Do you like that?" I asked.

His eyes fluttered as he bit his lower lip. "Yes," he grunted. "Fuck."

The head of his cock pressed against me. He gently lowered his hips, pushing inside of me.

I moaned, having not been stretched by another in so long. My fingers dug into the blankets as I took him, my channel pulsing around him, gripping him like a vice.

"Oh gods," he rasped. "You feel so fucking good, Moss."

He looked up, his eyes meeting mine through his lashes. Glitter still swathed his smooth skin, his moans blending with mine as he thrust all the way in.

I cried out and he froze. "No," I grunted. "No, don't stop. Fuck me, little *tarax*."

His eyes flashed with need and he let out a low grunt, looking down as he started to fuck me, watching his cock push in and out with every movement. I writhed beneath him, feeling the vibrations through my body.

I'd never been in heat before but I knew, theoretically, the stages we would go through. And soon, we'd settle into the fire of our fever, followed by orgasms that would vibrate through both of us simultaneously.

If I came, he would come. If he came, I would.

"I have things to tell you about this heat," I huffed.

He shook his head as he fucked me harder, his cock throbbing within me. "I'm here for it all, whatever happens. I can't think while I fuck you."

I let out a soft laugh, but I could barely think either. Harder and harder, he pumped into me, his grunts turning me on. My tentacle tightened around his balls, squeezing them gently, urging his cum to fill me soon.

I needed him to. The ferocity of that desire made me gasp.

"Come inside me," I begged. "Please. I need you to fill me with your come. I need to feel it within me. *Please, Max.*"

He let out a long groan, his hips snapping against mine faster. I knew he was on the edge. I could feel it, the pleasure swelling before both of us.

Max gasped, giving one final thrust. He buried his cock deep inside me, my moan mirroring his own as he came. I felt his hot cum shoot inside of me, filling me with every milky drop. His orgasm echoed through me, his pleasure my own. I drowned in it, my eyes closing as I felt him in me, around me, with me.

He made a soft noise, wavering slightly. I reached up, cupping his face, our eyes meeting again.

"I can't find the right words to describe how I feel." He made a face, his breaths turning into pants. His cock hardened inside of me again. "This is crazy. I've never felt this way before."

Crazy was a very human word for it, but it made me smile.

"The *haze*," I whispered.

We called it a haze. The heat induced euphoric rush after an orgasm was amplified and shared between us, creating an intense effect that was a sort of high. I breathed in his scent, the taste of my own cum still on my tongue. I licked my lips as I felt the heat of his cum inside of me, pushing deeper.

Part of me wished he would impregnate me. I let out a low hum, the thought surprising me. I wondered what a child between us would look like.

Just the heat, I lied to myself. That desire was just from our heat. The breeding desire was so strong, but I wasn't even sure a human and arborian could create offspring.

Max gave a soft thrust again. "This is a different type of torture," he murmured. "I can't stop."

"Don't," I huffed. "Don't fight yourself."

He leaned down and pressed a kiss against my lower abs as he moved his hips, drawing his cock back before pushing into me again. He reached between us, his fingertips finding that sweet nub again.

I covered my mouth with my hand before my shout could wake the entire city.

My love. My pollinai.

I squeezed my eyes shut as tears formed, the pleasure overwhelming me. It was too much. It was too much, and yet not enough to cure this infernal affliction.

He pumped into me gentler this time, every movement hard and measured, all while he circled my clit. My tentacles writhed as he took me, wanting to be back inside of him.

Later. Later. I promised myself.

We couldn't stop yet. We couldn't stop now. We'd fuck in every position before we had a moment of clarity.

He continued to kiss my body as he fucked me. I laid there, feeling every emotion combined with the purest sort of pleasure.

"Moss?" he whispered. "Come with me."

He circled my clit harder as he drove into me, our orgasms mounting and mounting until again—we came together, hitting the crescendo with such a passion that I forgot who I was for a moment.

He collapsed against me. I ran my fingers through his hair, holding him against my body.

We were so different. In so many ways.

And yet the universe had brought us together tonight, and for the next few nights in a way that was beyond either of our understanding.

"I can feel your emotions," he said softly. "Are you sad?"

"No," I whispered. "I'm in awe."

He gave a gentle nod, his arms wrapping around me as best as they could.

"I want to fuck you in the springs," I mumbled.

His head snapped up and he raised a brow. Again, his cock stiffened inside of me.

"Are you in pain?" I teased him.

"No," he snorted. "You were right about this heat changing things. I feel like I've taken *super-v*, which is a drug for staying hard..."

"Pull out of me slowly and I'll fuck you in the spring."

"Such a romantic," he teased.

I could be. I loved being romantic. I panicked for a moment as he gently eased out of me, wondering if I should have done something different. I hadn't courted him, I hadn't even gifted him anything.

All those things, I still could do.

But not until this heat was finished.

Until then, he was trapped in my arms and riding my cocks.

He slid off me and grabbed my hand, tugging me off the bed. I rolled off quickly and made him squeal as I lifted him, throwing him over my shoulder. His cum dripped down my thighs as I carried him down the hall to the spring.

"I love your horns," he murmured.

"My horns?"

"Yes."

"They can bring me pleasure, you know..."

Max let out a noise of surprise as I stepped into the spring room.

"Well, I think we should explore that, don't you?"

CHAPTER 5
Purple Haze

MAX

I'd had sex plenty of times in my life, but nothing had ever been like this. Being with Moss felt like an elemental pairing—the two of us tumbling together in a dance of give and take.

Xe lowered me into the hot springs, the water swirling around us. There were particles of light that seemed to move with the ripples we made, reminding me of the bioluminescent algae on certain beaches on Earth. I tipped my head back and looked at the ceiling, the thousands of crystals reflecting small images of us. And then there were the branches that wound through the walls, creating a cavern of natural beauty.

Moss pressed xyr lips to my shoulder, xyr hand sliding gently around my neck. It was a firm hold and one that turned me on more than I thought possible.

"Moss," I murmured, closing my eyes as xe touched me.

The pool was fairly deep. My feet couldn't touch the

bottom at the center, but that didn't matter since Moss held me close, xyr tentacles writhing against me.

All of the passion had simmered down into a tender smolder. Every touch left its mark as xe continued to explore me with xyr lips. I huffed and turned around, wrapping my legs around xyr waist. I reached up, running my palm over one of xyr many horns.

Moss let out a soft growl, almost like a purr. I felt it rumble through xyr chest. Xyr eyes seemed to change again, brightening into a shade of violet that stole my breath before darkening again.

"Your eyes," I whispered.

Xe nodded. "The colors change sometimes."

"Wow," I whispered reverently. "You are beautiful."

Moss blushed. "You think so?"

"I do," I murmured, pressing my lips to xyrs.

Xe kept smiling as xe kissed me. I sighed against xem, reaching up and knotting my fingers in xyr long hair. I felt the tip of one of the tentacles pressing against me again, my breath hitching as it pushed inside of me.

I arched, dragging in a gulp of air as I sank down, taking more of xem. "Fuck," I moaned.

The pleasure was unending. I shuddered around xem as we moved, our movements gentle. The water sloshed around us, the luminescent particles swirling.

"I could stay like this forever," Moss sighed.

I nodded, my cry ringing around us as the tentacle went deeper. The second one joined in, probing me gently before intertwining and thrusting into me.

I kissed down xyr neck, unable to resist the urge to bite xem. Moss let out a low growl as I sank my teeth into xyr skin, kissing and biting and leaving marks everywhere I could.

"Your little teeth are sharp," Moss chuckled, pumping into me harder.

"Bite me," I murmured. My cock hardened against xem at the thought of xem sinking xyr sharp teeth into me. "I like the pain."

"Do you?" xe purred.

Xe gripped the back of my head, pulling me back and exposing my neck. I whimpered as xe leaned in, just grazing my skin lightly, playfully. Driving me crazy.

"Moss," I moaned.

Xe chuckled. "Beg me."

I made a noise, somewhere between a growl and helpless groan. Xyr tentacles pumped inside of me, my cock throbbing between us.

"Please," I rasped. "Please, please, please bite me."

Xyr fangs brushed over my throat.

I bucked against xem, demanding it. "Please!"

"It'll hurt," xe whispered.

"*Fucking bite me.*"

Xe smiled against me. The tip of xyr tongue traced me slowly, teasing.

"*Moss,*" I cried. "I swear to the gods—"

Xyr fangs sank into my neck, the pain a sudden sharp contrast to the mindless pleasure flowing through both of us. I wasn't sure if I screamed, because the moment xe sank xyr fangs into me, I came so hard I lost myself to the feelings of everything.

Moss moaned as xe sucked. I could feel xyr cum inside of me, breeding me as xe bit down harder. Xyr nails raked down my back and I arched, crying out again.

Xe pulled xyr fangs free from me as xe panted. Blood wet xyr lips, swiped away by xyr tongue.

"Again," I rasped.

Moss growled and lifted me, pulling xyr tentacles free. Xe carried me to the edge of the pool and bent me over it, shoving inside of me again as xe leaned over my body and sank xyr fangs into my shoulder.

I screamed again, tears blurring my vision. "Fuck!" I shouted, but I wanted more. I needed more.

I'd succumbed to the haze between us and didn't want it to end. The tentacles fucked me relentlessly, moving in and out as Moss bit down, marking me as xyrs. I felt like xyr sex toy, xyr strength of holding me and using me turning me on in a new way. I liked the feeling of being fucked like this, my body held with ease as xe thrusted in and out.

Xe released me, xyr tongue swiping over the bite marks eagerly. "They'll heal quickly," Moss murmured, licking them again.

"Means you can bite me more, then?" I huffed.

Moss snorted. "If you like pain, I have other devices too."

I glanced over my shoulder, my eyes widening. I was curious about what xe meant.

"I'm going to fill you again and then we'll wash off and I'll take you to bed," Moss said. "You need some rest, even if only for a couple hours."

"Maybe you'll fuck me while I sleep," I whispered.

Moss growled, thrusting xyr hips. "Would you like me too?"

"Yes," I admitted, grunting as xe fucked me harder. "I want to wake up to you using me. However you want."

"I can do that," Moss groaned. "Are you certain?"

"I'm more than certain."

That had been a desire of mine for so long, one that I'd never asked for but with Moss it felt like an easy request. All of the kinks I'd never indulged in came to the surface, my thoughts wandering as Moss gave one last pump, filling me again with xyr cum.

Xe braced xyr hands on the sides of the pool, breathing hard. I felt the lull, and knew xe did too. A few moments of clarity between the lust.

Moss kissed the back of my neck and then eased out. "You're perfect, little *tarax*."

"What is a *tarax*?" I asked.

Xe chuckled and moved across the pool, stepping out briefly and then returning with what appeared to be a bath bomb. They tossed it into the pool and it began to fizzle.

"This will clean our bodies," Moss said. "*Tarax* is a sort of flower that blooms rarely in an oasis. You remind me of its scent. It's a beautiful flower, and my favorite too."

I blushed as I turned and pressed my back against the pool's wall, finding a ledge to sit on. Moss met my gaze and offered me a soft smile.

"I can think for a moment," I said.

"For a moment, as can I."

I swallowed hard because all I could think about was how I wanted to know xem more.

Moss stepped to the center of the pool and lowered completely, xyr horns disappearing beneath the water. I could still see the orange tips beneath the surface.

I decided to do the same and dipped below, running my fingers through my hair. The water tingled against my skin, cooling me despite the fact that it was a hot spring. I rose back up, wiping my eyes as Moss emerged too.

"Your hair is so long," I said in awe. "Do...do you have a brush? Would you like me to brush it?"

Moss stared at me for a moment and then xyr expression melted. "If you wish to," xe whispered, xyr voice hoarse.

"Is that okay?" I asked. "Is that something I shouldn't have asked?"

"It's very intimate," Moss explained. "But I would like for you to after you drink water and eat something."

As if on cue, my stomach grumbled. I had no idea what time it was, but this had to be one of the longest days I'd ever had.

"Food, water, hair brushing, sleep, and fucking," I said, making a list.

Moss smiled and nodded, going to the steps of the pool and rising out. I admired xyr body as I swam to the steps, following xem. Moss shook xyr body in a way that I certainly could not, xyr skin drying completely, but leaving xyr hair still damp.

"I can't dry like that," I snorted.

"Oh. Hmm. Let me find a cloth. Stay here." Moss disappeared beyond the doorway for a moment and then came back holding a clean robe that belonged to xem. "This will do I think."

I smiled as xe wrapped me in it, drying me off quickly. I breathed in xyr scent, closing my eyes with a soft hum.

I could feel the exhaustion starting to hit now. Beneath it, there was the horny buzz again, but...

Xe scooped me up and carried me down the hall to xyr kitchen. Xe sat me on the countertop as xe got me water, bringing me a glass. I drank it as xe rummaged for food.

"I don't know what humans eat," Moss mumbled.

"What do Arborians eat?" I asked.

"Mostly plants and fish. Ah, here's something that might work."

Xe pulled out a pack wrapped in silver with faint writing on it. I wasn't going to ask how long that had been in xyr cabinet. I took the pack and raised a brow, checking the date. It was a bar that would certainly fill me up until tomorrow, something we carried a lot of on the ship. I opened the wrapper and bit into it, surprised by how fresh it still tasted.

"Tomorrow, I will order a banquet," Moss said. "If that is okay."

"Yes," I said. "We can fuck and eat and drink all day tomorrow. My next rehearsal won't be for a couple days. This worked out well."

"Good. I'll need to call my work tomorrow, but they'll understand."

"Will you tell them what happened?" I asked, curious.

"Yes. To go into *sporev* is involuntary. I'll have my time off. They will function perfectly fine without me."

I ate and drank my water quickly and then followed Moss back to the bedroom. Moss grabbed what looked like a wooden comb, and handed it to me. The two of us sat on the bed, and I ran my fingers through xyr hair, feeling how silky the strands were. Xyr muscles were hard and defined, whereas xyr hair was long and soft, and absolutely stunning. I ran the comb through it, working everything gently.

Moss let out a happy sigh, humming as I continued to brush through every lock.

"Remember you can wake me up and fuck me," I teased as I finished brushing xyr hair.

I set the comb to the side and they took it, returning it to its place on xyr dresser.

"Time to sleep. Your body has to be exhausted, even with my cum inside of you and pheromones changing yours."

I grabbed the edge of the blankets and pulled them back, settling in. Moss crawled in next to me, pulling me close to xyr body. I buried my face against the crook of xyr neck, smiling against xem.

My stomach twisted with excitement. Ironically the thing that made me want to fall asleep was the idea of waking up to Moss fucking me.

Moss let out a soft growl. "Even now I can feel how dirty your mind is. Go to sleep, little *tarax*."

I smirked, but xe was right.

I closed my eyes and breathed in xyr scent. I'd had one of the best nights of my life between my first performance and Moss.

I was a real burlesque performer now.

I let that sink in and soon was drifting towards the stars.

CHAPTER 6

MOSS

Listening to a human sleep was a new experience for me. It wasn't my sleep cycle yet so I laid next to Max for a couple hours, listening to his soft snores with a stupid smile on my face. My body heated on and off, the fever creeping up and my willpower controlled by just a thread of strength.

Max needed his sleep. I would wake him later, but for now...

I breathed him in and then gently slid out of bed, careful not to wake him. I grabbed my night robe and slid it on. I left my room and crept quietly down the hall to my small office, shutting the door carefully behind me. My tentacles writhed freely, already being away from him making me tense.

I just needed to send some messages off and then I'd go back to bed. I sat down and the communications system came on, the sheer amount of notifications making me sigh.

I pressed my finger to the pad on my desk and the screen came up, a virtual space that gleamed in the dark.

"Open notifications," I commanded.

I had a message from the council and then several messages from Dio. I scowled and clicked on one of them, feeling a series of alarm bells through my mind.

Attention Moss:
Why are you pushing through funds for the Galactic Gems?? We shouldn't be responsible for their damages! I handled everything perfectly well, but you interfered!

WHY DID YOU GO TO THEIR SHOW?
Dio

He was clearly furious that I'd gone to the Galactic Gems show.

A string of curses left me as I kept reading. That message was just one of several.

"What is going on?" I whispered, scowling.

I couldn't understand why this was setting him off so much. Dio was fairly new to my team, and I didn't appreciate the way he was responding to this.

I shook my head and opened up a fresh message, including all of Dio's messages as an attachment to the council for approval for reprimand. I sent it off, and then started another message, notifying them of my *sporev* and that when I returned, I would follow up on Dio and the payments owed to the burlesque troupe.

My lips pressed together as I waited for a response. I read a couple more of Dio's messages, all of which were angrier and angrier. Especially since I hadn't responded to him.

And I certainly wouldn't respond through messages. Not with that tone.

The council response was quick and brief: enjoy my time and don't worry about anything else.

I rolled my shoulders and leaned back in my chair, already thinking about Max again. The idea that Dio was so up in arms about me supporting the troupe made my own hackles rise. Dio had never been violent before, though, so I tried to calm myself.

My tentacles throbbed. In fact, my entire body felt like it was falling apart. I groaned and rose, leaving the office and going back to my bedroom, following Max's scent like a bloodhound. I paused in the doorway, watching as his bare chest rose and fell.

I stifled a groan. My mouth watered and I couldn't resist from sliding off my robe and taking a seat in the corner of my bedroom. I could see him perfectly from here.

Sario. I bit my lower lip. The memory of his blood came back to me, taunting that primal, monstrous part that dwelled within, waiting to consume and mate again.

Max. His name drilled through me as I slid my hand around the base of my upper tentacle, gripping myself and stroking. The suckers pulled at my palm, leaving soft kisses as I moved up and down, wishing that he was kneeling before me.

The thought alone of him before me, his sweet mouth sucking...

"*Sario,*" I huffed.

I didn't want to wake him yet. I closed my eyes, my heavy head falling back as I kept stroking myself.

A soft whimper fluttered through the room.

My eyes flew open and I stared at Max. He still appeared to be asleep, but that sound...

Curious, I stood and went to the edge of the bed, peering

down at him. Another moan parted his lips, his breaths quickening as he moved in his sleep.

Was he *dreaming*?

I'd heard that humans could have very vivid dreams, images that played in their brains during sleep. I could hardly imagine it, as I'd never had such a thing happen to me.

The blankets rested around his hips, his chest bare. I fought the urge to touch him, but was quickly losing the battle.

He'd told me he wanted to wake up being used.

My tentacles throbbed with need. I sucked in a breath, feeling my will crumble with every second that passed.

I reached for one of his nipples, circling it gently with my fingertip. His scent was potent as I continued to play with him, teasing each nipple until his breath hitched. My gaze slid down to the blanket and the bulge lifting it.

I couldn't stop now. I shivered, trying to keep my movements quiet as I went around the bed and carefully climbed back in. I settled in next to him, but he didn't stir.

I slid my arm beneath his back and tugged and turned him in the same moment, spooning my body against his. He adjusted, but then his breathing deepened.

I waited until I was certain he was asleep.

Precum lubed my tentacles. I craved him in every moment of my existence.

Carefully, I pressed my body against him and lifted his thighs lightly. Already, my tentacles reached for him, one curling around his balls while the other probed his entrance.

A long moan left him in his sleep.

"Keep dreaming, little *tarax*," I huffed.

My tentacle was lubed up enough that the tip slipped in. I moved slowly, grunting as I carefully rocked my hips against his ass.

I closed my eyes, drinking in the feel of his body pulsing

around me, gripping me as I slid in and out. I worked him gently, a low growl rumbling in my chest as I took him.

"Can you feel me?" I whispered so quietly I was sure he couldn't hear me. "Can you feel your mate fucking you?"

Mate.

I felt a flash of terror. The word has slipped out so seamlessly, and it didn't feel wrong. In fact, it felt right.

It was too soon for that. Too soon to know.

I whimpered, my control loosening the longer I was inside of him.

"Max," I whispered hoarsely.

What was he doing to me? I was unraveling just from his touch, from being inside of him and knowing that he wanted this. I thrust harder, panting as I took him.

His moan came louder and I felt his muscles tense, his body starting to stir.

I growled and flipped him over onto his stomach, mounting him from behind as he gasped, crying out as I thrust into him entirely.

"Fuck," he whimpered sleepily. "*Yes.* Fuck me."

His sleepy murmurs sent me over the edge. I fucked him harder, groaning as I took him over and over, invading him repeatedly.

He bucked against the bed, his body trembling beneath me.

I could do this forever with him. I felt the full force of my heat flooding back as I fucked him, pleasure rolling through my body in immense waves. Euphoria wrapped around me, his body taking me.

I leaned down, kissing down his spine as my tentacles thrust in and out of him.

"Moss," he cried. "Fuck! Harder!"

"Any harder and I might break the bed," I growled.

"Break it," he rasped.

My muscles rippled with strength. I reached up, bracing my hand against the headboard as I took him. He grunted and I felt his orgasm rush through me and *shatter* me.

Pushing me to the edge.

I couldn't stop myself. With a guttural shout, I thrust into him once more, filling him as I came.

He gasped, writhing beneath me. I held him in place, closing my eyes.

"Gods," he murmured sleepily. He let out a dark chuckle and relaxed beneath me. "Wake me up like that always, hmm?"

"Are you okay?" I asked.

"Am I okay? I was having a dream about you breeding me and woke up with your tentacle cocks in my ass. Yes, I'm more than okay. I'm splendid."

"*Splendid.*" I echoed.

What a strange word. He turned his head, looking up at me with a grin.

"You dirty little slut," I teased, kissing his cheek.

"I certainly am," he said as thrust his hips back.

I let out a low growl. I pulled out of him and sat back as he rolled to the side, revealing his cum smeared against his throbbing cock and stomach.

I leaned down before he could protest, swiping my tongue over the milky liquid. He buried his fingers into the blankets as I licked up every drop, hungry for more.

The taste of his cum was like a drug for me right now.

"Oh," he whimpered as I took his cock into my mouth.

I settled on the bed as I sucked him, determined to stay like this for a while. He surprised me as he reached up and stroked one of my horns.

Pleasure rippled through me. My eyes rolled back.

"We never explored that," he rasped. "Fuck, if you keep sucking me, I'm going to cum."

I pulled my lips off for a moment, but only a moment. "I need to drink your seed from your cock."

"Oh."

His cock hardened even more in my grip as I started to suck him again. He began to stroke my horns, touching each of the many tips and playing with them, gripping them like cocks.

He sat up as much as he could and shocked me yet again by sucking the tip of one.

Sario.

I was a goner.

I reached up and grabbed a pillow, lifting my hips and placing it against my tentacles. I humped against it as I sucked his cock and he sucked and licked my horns.

"Fuck," he mumbled. "You're so hot when you're feral."

I was. I was absolutely feral. I humped the pillow harder, whimpering as I took him as deep as possible, his balls resting against my chin. I breathed in his scent—that sweet, addictive, mind-blowing scent—and growled.

He grabbed onto my horns, gripping them as I kept going. His moans and cries were musical, all while my hips kept thrusting and pumping.

"You're making me jealous of the pillow," he teased, his words ending on a long moan. "Fuck, I'm so close."

Come for me. Come for me, little tarax.

He gasped, his body stiffening beneath me. "I heard you!"

I felt a moment of shock too, but it wasn't enough for me to stop. If anything, it just pushed me on further.

"What the fuck?" he moaned, his grip tightening on my horns.

Fill me. Breed my mouth. I need to taste you.

"Moss," he whimpered. "Moss, I'm so close—*fuck!*"

Hot ropes of cum shot into my mouth, salty and thick. I swallowed everything, closing my eyes as I drowned myself in his taste. I gently pulled my lips off, panting.

I licked my lips as I kept humping the pillow.

Max made a soft growl, tugging my horns. "Inside me," he rasped. "If you come, it better be inside me."

"You're so demanding," I snarled playfully.

I lifted my hips and tossed the pillow to the side. I grabbed him and pulled him down, pushing his legs back and lining up my tentacles with his ass.

I shoved into him relentlessly. The bed squeaked beneath us as I pounded into him, pinning his arms above his head. I had the idea of tying him up and doing this, his eyes widened as if he had thought the same thing.

"You can hear my thoughts now," I panted.

"I think I can," he huffed. "Tying me up?"

I nodded, amazed. This meant...this meant that...

I covered the thought as best as I could, not wanting him to know. Not wanting him to know what I thought. I focused on fucking him, the feel of his body, his scents and tastes that sent me into this unending sexual frenzy.

My orgasm this time was softer and longer, dragging out as I came inside of him, emptying everything I had.

It felt like it would never end.

But I didn't want it to.

He grabbed my horn and dragged me down into a kiss, licking the inside of my mouth. "You taste like me," he whispered.

"Yes," I murmured, deepening our kiss.

I pulled my tentacles free and melted down against him, running my hands up and down his body as his legs wrapped around my waist.

Max was changing me. He let out a soft chuckle, wrapping his arms around my neck too.

"Sure you don't need any sleep?"

"No," I sighed. "But you need more. I'll keep my hands and tentacles to myself."

"Only for a little while. Wake me up again, hmm?"

He kissed me as I rolled off him, the two of us settling back into bed. It wasn't long before he was softly snoring again.

CHAPTER 7
Breakfast

MAX

I woke up to the smell of food and immediately raised my head, my stomach grumbling. After everything that we'd done last night, I'd certainly worked up an appetite.

Soft light drifted through Moss's bedroom, highlighting the leaves that sprouted above. I stared at the ceiling, following the tangle of branches. The homes on this planet simply amazed me. We were literally in a massive tree that housed countless others, full with amenities, a pool, electricity.

I could see why this was xyr favorite room, though. It was hard to choose between this and the bathroom.

I curled into the blankets, pulling them up to my shoulders as I rolled over, staying still for a moment. I was a little sore, but not nearly as much as I should have been between hours of fucking and an aerial performance.

A smile crept over my lips. I ran through the show last

night, my Galactic Gems debut. It had gone better than I could have expected. The rush was exhilarating.

I could live on stage forever. It was where I was meant to be.

To think I started out as just a stagehand. Some wild things had happened since I'd joined this troupe, especially being blamed for poisoning two performers, but they were like a family. And at least that situation had been taken care of.

Madam Moonie took a chance on me. I was determined to show up and prove that I was worthy of her confidence.

My stomach grumbled again, reminding me that I needed a heavy breakfast.

A shower, food, and Moss. Those were the three things I needed most.

My eyes drifted closed for a few more minutes before I finally forced myself to sit up. I shoved the blankets back as I got out of bed, groaning as I stretched. I bent over and stayed that way for a few moments, spreading out and working my muscles.

I went through a few yoga poses until I felt less stiff. I could hear Moss in the kitchen, the sound of utensils clanking against each other echoing through the home. I smiled to myself.

Xe is so cute.

And hot.

I breathed out. Those thoughts immediately turned more lustful.

Really, this had been one of the best twists in my life. Certainly better than being accused of poisoning people and then watching a performer be kidnapped by an alien cowboy who only, very exclusively, wore chaps.

It had been an interesting few months, but being with Moss? The heat we shared? That might have topped it all, but in the best way possible.

How much sex could an alien and human have? The galactic sky was the limit. All I could think about was touching and feeling xem.

I blew out a breath, rolled my shoulders again, and then crept to the doorway. I pressed my palm against the wooden frame, feeling how soft and smooth it was. I looked down the hall, catching a glimpse of violet and horns.

Before I launched myself at Moss, I needed to shower. While I didn't think xe would care about me being covered in xyr come, I sure did. I went down the hall quietly and slipped into the bathroom.

Aside from the glowing pool at the center, there was also a shower. I hadn't even noticed that last night in my sexual haze. I stepped beneath it and messed with the buttons until water rained down on me. I found soap, washed down, and stood there rubbing my shoulders and thinking about sucking Moss's tentacles.

My dirty mind. My cheeks flushed. It was like every little thing made me think about sex.

I finished rinsing off. The robe was hanging up again and I air dried for a few minutes before slipping it around myself.

Now, the scent of food made my mouth water. I left the bathroom and headed towards the kitchen, smiling as I spotted Moss.

I cleared my throat. "Morning," I said.

The scent of coffee wafted through the apartment, making me moan.

Moss looked up at me with a wide, pointed grin. "Morning," xe said. "I have coffee brewing if you would like a cup."

"More than you know," I said.

I went to the edge of the bar, leaning against it as xe poured me a cup and slid it towards me. The cup was as large as a bowl, reminding me of the size difference between the two of us.

"I am making some food for breakfast, and if you don't like it, we can order something," Moss said.

"Okay. Whatever it is, it smells delicious."

I found myself blushing as Moss slid xyr gaze over me, appreciating me. Drinking me in. My cock perked up, my heart hammering as I took a sip of coffee.

"How'd you sleep?" xe teased.

"Very well. And you?"

"I didn't sleep. I just laid there and went through a million different scenarios, all of which ended with me fucking you or you fucking me a million different ways."

"Oh."

Fuck.

I swallowed hard as Moss went back to a skillet that was sizzling over a stove top. I breathed out, trying to steady myself. How was I supposed to be able to think straight when xe said things like that?

"Drink your coffee," Moss purred.

"Everything you say and do turns me on."

"Yes and I plan to take advantage of that once you're fed. And I suppose it wouldn't hurt to check in with your friends, hmm?"

I licked my lips. "Deal."

I kept sipping my coffee and decided xe was right. I slipped off the barstool and spent about ten minutes trying to find my phone. Ultimately, the slender device was tucked away in my bag. The moment I touched it, it began to ding and ding, messages alerting me, most of them from social media networks. The show had been a raging success last night, and some of the photos our photographers grabbed were stunning.

Seeing myself on the stage stole my breath. I took it back to the counter with my coffee.

"You can sync to my system, if you'd like," Moss said.

"Okay," I said.

"*Astar, sync,*" xe commanded.

My phone synced with the system, which allowed a holographic screen to pop up in the kitchen and show all of the photos. Moss made a surprised noise, grinning.

"Look how stunning you are."

I blushed. "I'm happy with it."

"And that was truly your first concert?"

"*Show.* Yes, it was," I said.

Moss nodded as xe plated food for us both. Xe brought the plates and utensils over, sitting across from me. The screen moved, still showing us more photos. Some of Stella, of Lady Luna, Milky Maid, and others. A couple of backstage photos caught Moss and me too.

"Oh," I said. "I can ask them to delete those, if you'd prefer."

Moss paused it on a photo of the two of us looking at each other. My cheeks flushed, my body language stiff but only because I'd been fighting a hard-on for hours. And the way Moss looked at me.

"No, I like this," xe said. "I like this a lot. Eat your food, little *tarax*. You need sustenance."

I stuck my tongue out at xem, but took a bite of my food. The flavors burst on my tongue, slightly spicy and earthy but utterly delicious. I groaned, digging in as more notifications flashed across the screen. I wasn't surprised to see Madam Moonie's message and sent her a quick one back, a sign of life that she would appreciate.

"Oh, did you need to check in with work?" I asked, remembering xe had mentioned so in passing.

"I already did," Moss chuckled. "They told me to take care and not to worry about work. And I won't, even with the difficulties of this week."

"Is that related to the damages?" I asked.

"Yes and no. One of our employees made the situation worse, and they ended up sending me some threatening messages about the entire situation. I don't understand why they would do so, but I forwarded it to the council and will deal with it later."

I pressed my lips together, feeling a flicker of worry. "Did they threaten you?" I asked.

Moss leaned forward, xyr gaze holding mine. In it, I felt like I could see the entire universe gazing back at me, holding all of my wonders and hopes in a thousand shades of violet. I got lost for a moment, and then came back to the present.

Don't worry about me, Moss's voice sounded through my mind.

I sucked in a shocked breath. Hearing a voice echo through my mind was a very new experience. It was deep and personal and I loved it, having this new connection that went beyond any sort of technology our worlds possessed.

"Fine," I mumbled. "But if they do threaten you, you have to tell me. Because that's not okay."

"My love, and what would you do? You are half the size of an Arborian."

"I'm small but mighty. I'd rip them a new asshole."

Moss burst out laughing and I smiled, even though I was serious. I was ready to fist fight anyone that threatened my...

I swallowed hard. My what?

My partner? My lover?

My mate?

I felt a deep yearning curl through me, winding around my heart, a ribbon tugged tight. I bit my tongue though, because it felt silly and embarrassing to assume such a thing. Even if the thought of being with Moss forever already appealed to me in a lovesick way, I just...

"You are thinking so hard," Moss teased. "What about?"

"Oh nothing," I said.

I cleared my throat and kept eating, trying to steer my thoughts back to the moments in front of me. I looked up at Moss, admiring xyr horns and face and long, silky hair. Xe was absolutely beautiful. Gold gleamed around xyr neck, and detailed the robes xe wore.

"Does your necklace mean something?" I asked.

Moss reached up and touched it, nodding. "Yes. It's an heirloom from my lineage, and a symbol of power within the community."

"But aren't you just a manager for travel and things?"

"Well, I am. But I am also a member of the planetary council."

"Oh." That was way more than I'd realized. "Like the entire planet?"

"Yes," Moss chuckled. "The whole planet."

"So like Toras or Zin, who are both Stella's mates. Zin is the Lazulian prince and Toras is a chancellor."

"Yes and no. I am not royalty and I don't represent the planet outside of our system. I oversee transportation and do help with guiding tourists and such. It's a very large council, and it's democratic in the sense that we are voted in. It's just, many members of my family have been on this council in the past."

"Interesting," I whispered. "How many people live on Arbor?"

"Only three billion on Arbor. But, our lives last much longer, and our reproductive habits are not the same as humans."

"That's still so many," I said. "So I'm in heat with an Arborian official."

"And I'm in heat with a burlesque star," Moss teased.

I found myself leaning closer. I reached for Moss's hand, sliding my palm against xyrs. "I think that if you don't fuck me soon, I will simply perish."

Xe smirked. "I need you to be fed and watered first, or you *will* perish."

"Don't threaten me with a good time," I mumbled.

I finished eating and drinking my coffee, and then snorted as Moss thrust a glass of water in front of me too, waiting ever so patiently for me to finish.

The longer I sat here, the more I wondered what xe had in store for me.

I raised a brow as I finished my water. "Happy?"

"Satisfied."

"Are you?"

Moss's eyes darkened as xe gave me a wicked smile. "Little *tarax*. Are you grumpy I didn't wake you by fucking you again?"

"Maybe," I mumbled.

"Such a travesty. Stand up."

Xyr tone went straight to my cock. I swallowed hard as I slid off the barstool and stood, waiting to see what xe would ask next.

"Good. Strip for me."

I smirked. Stripping? I could do that all day. I teased Moss as I pulled back the robe, exposing my shoulder before spinning around, shimmying it down my back.

Moss was patient as I worked it down my body until I was completely naked. I dropped the fabric to the floor. I shook my ass, looking over my shoulder at xem.

"Bend over."

I grunted and did as xe asked, but very slowly. Painfully slowly.

"Good. All the way. Spread your legs."

My cock was hard now as I spread my legs further for xem.

"Very good. Stay like that until I tell you to move."

Oh gods.

Every second that went by, I grew more and more horny.

How long was Moss going to leave me this way?

CHAPTER 8
Obey

MOSS

Nothing could have prepared me for the way Max's frustration that I had yet to touch him turned me on. I sat patiently, watching as he waited so obediently for me, bent over and ready to take me.

The heat was burning me alive, but this? Watching him struggle to do such a simple task because he wanted me so much? It was worth the painful flames coursing through my veins, burning me up from the inside as I drank him in.

Only Max could cool me, satiate me, and entice me in such a way.

"Moss," he rasped.

My gaze roamed over his body. The body that had taken me last night over and over. The one that I wanted to worship, devour, and love. I mentally cupped his asscheeks, a low growl leaving me as I imagined all of the things I wanted to do to him.

"I'm dying here," he grunted.

"You and me both."

He stiffened for a moment and then relaxed again.

I rose from the stool quietly, but I didn't go to him. Even as he let out a helpless whimper.

My dark purple robes slid to the floor, my tentacles writhing as I slid my hand down, stroking them. Readying them. The suckers exuded clear liquid, desperate to be buried inside of him.

But not yet.

The tension in the room was thick. Morning light painted a picturesque image, highlighting his bright orange hair and golden skin. I could still see a few flecks of glitter stuck to his skin, gleaming like tiny jewels.

I rolled my shoulders back, looking down at my body.

I needed to touch him.

His breath hitched as I came around the counter, stopping behind him. Only inches separated us, but within that short distance, there was the buzz of carnal anticipation.

We had all day. All day to fuck and kiss and make love over and over before reality found us tomorrow. Our heat was moving fast and I wanted to savor every single moment with him.

"I don't want it to end," I whispered softly.

Max understood what I meant. He let out a soft grunt, pressing his palms against the floor as he waited for me. "I don't either, but I'm dying here. I need you, Moss."

"I know," I murmured.

I stepped closer, running my hand over his hip. The moment our skin touched, there was a static charge, his lust rushing over me. I moaned, tilting my head back as I felt everything. I let him feel me too, knowing that my own desires were washing over him, bathing him in our lustful fire.

"*Please*," he begged.

His voice was so soft. So sweet.

I pressed my hips against his, holding on as I rubbed my tentacles against him.

Sario.

I couldn't fight my desires. Edging him was edging myself. It was hard to keep myself from immediately thrusting inside of him.

Instead, I reached around, leaning over him as I tweaked his nipples. He gasped, bucking against me.

"Fuck," he moaned.

"Did I say you could move yet?" I growled.

The sound he made was delicious. He remained bent over as the tip of my tentacle began to circle his hole, the liquid exuded from the suckers lubing him.

Pleasure gripped me. I tilted my head back, savoring the feeling of him. The tentacle kept stroking him, working him, readying him to take more.

I could do this forever.

I could stay in bed fucking him over and over forever.

The second tentacle gently wrapped around his balls, squeezing and fondling them.

"*Fuck, fuck,*" he rasped. "*Please.*"

"Are *fuck* and *please* all you can say?" I teased as I thrust into him.

He cried out, his voice chiming around us.

"Yes," he moaned. "That's all I can fucking...*fuck.*"

I growled, not holding back. I held onto his hips as I started to pump into him, breeding his little hole the way I'd wanted to for hours.

"Good boy," I panted. "You're squeezing me so tight."

"*Moss,*" he moaned.

"Too much?"

"No," he rasped.

I smiled, holding him firmly in place as I took him harder. The sound of our skin slapping against each other echoed in a firm rhythm, and I was practically holding him in the air with each thrust. I reached down and grabbed his hair, pulling him back to standing.

He gasped as I tugged him against my chest, my hand slipping around his throat as I lifted him, holding him in the air as I kept fucking him. My other arm clasped firmly around his stomach, bracing him as I took him.

"Mine," I snarled, breathing in his scent. My mouth watered as I said the word. "You're all mine."

"I'm yours. I'm yours."

I groaned again, enjoying the way he said that. It almost made me come, just knowing he was saying he belonged to me, but I was determined to hold out longer.

Euphoric pleasure enraptured me. My blood sang in my veins, my tentacled cocks wanting more.

The second tentacle released his balls and I pulled out, thrusting both in at the same time. He groaned, his hands clasping around my wrist, his nails digging in as I went deeper.

I pumped in and out, moving my hips at a rapid place.

I was so close.

So fucking close.

Not yet.

Maybe it was cruel and sadistic, but right as I came to the edge, and could feel him at the edge too, I pulled out, panting hard.

I released him, putting him back on his feet.

"What?" Max whimpered. He spun around, his breathing hard. "What are you doing?"

"Not yet," I told him.

"Fuck. I was so fucking close," he pouted.

I smiled, even if it was almost painful to stop. Edging him was edging myself too, but I was enjoying pushing the two of us.

I tipped his chin up, both of us still panting. "More soon. But not yet. Waiting will make it more explosive, right?"

"Maybe, but fuck. I don't know if I can hold out."

"I think you can," I teased.

He squeaked as I lifted him, throwing him over my shoulder.

I carried him down the hall to the bedroom. He squirmed against me, cursing me.

"You can't just fuck me and then..."

"Not let you come?" I asked.

I couldn't help but smirk.

"Yes," he huffed.

He let out a little growl as I stepped inside and went to another door, a closet. A human growling had to be one of the cutest things I'd ever heard.

"I have some toys that might interest you," I said. "You might find me teasing you worth it."

I could feel his cock throbbing against me.

"Moss, you're killing me," he moaned.

"I know, I know but we have all day."

"Oh gods, you can't edge me all day."

I smirked. "I can sure try."

I put him down and turned him so that he'd actually look at what was in the closet before jumping me. Max made a noise of surprise and stepped in, eyeing all of the toys that I had.

The closet was more of an extra room. I kept my robes in here, but aside from clothing, there were the restraints, floggers, and vibrating toys.

It just so happened that there were some very interesting

kink items out there in the universe. Some of the other aliens were very ingenious with their BDSM inventions.

"Someone is into restraints," Max teased, reaching up to run his fingers over some of the chains and leather restraints. He eyed some of the vibrating toys and then even reached up to touch a pump that would fit over my clit. "And okay, while I am still frustrated I haven't come yet, I am interested in all of this. What do you want to do to me today?"

He turned around and looked up, his expression making me melt. He slowly knelt in front of me, still keeping his eyes locked with mine.

"Does this please you?" he whispered. "Submission?"

"Yes," I breathed out.

"Did you like it when I did what you said earlier? Holding myself as long as I could?"

"Yes."

"Do you want to do more of that?"

"Only if you want to as well," I said. "I have *things* that I enjoy."

"You and me both. It's just we were a little too busy last night to get into *this* territory of things."

"We were," I whispered. I held his gaze a moment longer and then cleared my throat. "We should talk through everything first."

"Can you do that while I suck you?"

"No," I hissed. "You think I can think straight with your mouth around me?"

"No," Max snickered.

I held out my hand and helped him up, drawing him to the bed. The two of us climbed on and I turned onto my side, facing him.

"Well, I think it might be somewhat universal now, but we could use the red light system," Max said. "Green is good, yellow means check in, red means stop. Or we could use a safe word."

"Yes," I said. I was familiar with doing things either way. It had been awhile since I'd been with someone in this manner, which only made everything more exciting. I was eager to know about what Max enjoyed. "Either could work. But tell me what you enjoy."

Max slid closer to me and then turned on his side too. I licked my lips, admiring him as he spoke. "Well. With the right person, I like being submissive. I enjoy sensory deprivation. I like electrical play. I like the idea of you restraining me and doing terrible *wonderful* things. I enjoy pain, too."

All of those ideas excited me. I let out a low, hungry growl. Now that I could think a little clearer, it was easier to plan doing something like that with Max. Last night, I'd barely been able to think for a second without wanting to be inside of him or him inside of me. But now, we could savor these moments. The flaming heat had turned to a delicious smolder, and I wanted to enjoy every part of it.

"What safe word would you like to use?" I asked.

"I think red should work," he said. "Is that okay?"

"It is. And when you say s*ensory deprivation*—describe what that means to you."

He raised a brow and smiled. "It means maybe you blindfold me and muffle my hearing so I can't tell what's about to happen. Or maybe you control my breathing."

"Human necks are so fragile," I teased, sliding my hand up his chest.

"They are," he rasped. "But, I trust you."

"I know how to choke you, darling," I murmured.

"Prove it," he teased.

I raised a brow as I slid my hand around his neck, which was slender in my grip. I applied light pressure to the sides as his cheeks bloomed dark red. His pulse thrummed against my palm, a hummingbird-like beat.

He nodded. "Yes."

I released him, a low growl rumbling through my chest. Already, I wanted to do more.

"We'll use red as your safe word. And if you need me to slow down, you'll ask me to. Yes?"

"Yes," he whispered. "Of course."

"Good. Now get in the center of the bed and spread yourself out like a good boy."

CHAPTER 9

High

MAX

The anticipation was *killing* me.

I spread out on the bed as Moss grabbed restraints from xyr closet. My cock was hard and I was getting restless again, but I knew this was just the beginning.

Because I had been so focused on my career and becoming a burlesque dancer, I hadn't been with someone in this way in a very long time. I loved being submissive. I enjoyed being kinky. And I was excited to see what Moss had in store for me.

Especially with the range of toys in xyr closet.

I couldn't take my gaze off of xem. Xyr back faced me, xyr horns, gleaming, and sunlight as xe chose xyr devices. Xe came back to the bed, offering me a soft, wicked smile.

I blew out a breath, trying to control myself. All I wanted was for xem to fuck me more, and to make me come. But I also wanted to be tied down and used.

I wanted to beg xem.

The edging xe had done in the living room had killed me. I'd been so close to having one of the best orgasms ever, and then xe had stopped. All of that frustration was building, edging, turning me on as I waited for xyr touch.

"Are you ready?" xe asked.

"Yes."

Xe was so sexy. I couldn't look away from xyr beauty as xe came to me. I bit my lower lip as Moss lifted my wrist, sliding a cuff around it.

The restraint set was modern in many ways—there was a soft click and suddenly my arm was stretched as it autoconnected to the corner of the bed, not pulling too tight but also not too loose.

I was certainly not going anywhere.

The wonders of technology and sex toy evolution.

Xe did the same to my ankles and other wrist until I was spread out before xem, unable to do anything.

I was at xyr mercy.

"Look how sexy you look," Moss said, admiring me.

Every time xe looked at me like that, I felt myself melt. Xyr violet gaze raked over me, my cock throbbing.

"Sexy," xe whispered. "Stay put."

Xyr chuckle was devious. Moss returned to the closet, rummaging through items.

I heard the familiar zap of electricity.

"Oh gods," I whispered.

I raised my head, watching xem intently as xe returned to the bed with what looked like a sharp pinwheel, only when xe pressed a button, it shimmered with electricity.

"What is that?" I rasped.

"A very fun little invention," Moss said seriously. "It bites."

Fuck. I'd signed up for this, though. And while I felt a bolt of fear roll through me, that fear also made me feel hot.

I sucked in a breath as xe lowered the instrument, hovering above my skin.

"Moss," I groaned.

Sweat broke out over my skin. Xe hadn't even touched me yet, but not knowing what to expect was both terrifying and a turn on.

Moss was clearly pleased. Xe smirked deviously as xe lowered the toy. I gasped as I felt an electric shock run through me, but it wasn't as sharp as I had initially expected. Xe rolled the spiked wheel gently up my leg and it became more intense the longer it stayed on my skin.

I cried out as xe came closer to my cock.

Xe eased up my hip and then lifted, leaning over me to run the wheel over my chest. I moaned, my cock pulsing. Xe reached down with one hand, gripping me as xe continued to roll the electrical device over my body.

I thrust up, my breath hitching as desire, pain, and pleasure all mixed together.

Xe stroked me faster and faster.

"Are you trying to make me come?" I rasped helplessly.

I was so fucking close already. All of this edging was going to be the end of me. How long was xe going to do this to me?

I moaned and right as I was about to tip over the edge, Moss released me.

"Fuck," I snarled, straining against the cuffs. "Fuck you!"

Moss *laughed*.

"You're so mean," I gasped.

"Maybe a little bit..."

This side of Moss shocked and pleased me.

"You're at my mercy," Moss said. "The mercy of an alien that could turn you to dust..."

I raised a brow at xem. "To dust, huh?"

"Mmhmm. You're going nowhere, little *tarax*."

I yanked against the restraints as hard as I could, my muscles straining as I fought them.

But xe was right.

It was no use. I wasn't going anywhere. I let out another groan as Moss continued to play with me. Xe dragged the electric pinwheel down my chest, circling my nipples.

Electric pricks scattered through me, darting across my skin and zapping me.

I kept whimpering and moaning, sounds drawn out of me as I was shocked over and over.

I gasped as xe ran the utensil over my nipple.

"Fuck," I said again.

Xe let out a dark chuckle. Seeing xem look at me this way turned me on too. There was a wicked darkness there, a sensual edge that drove me mad.

Xe grabbed my cock again, stroking me gently. Precum dripped from the tip, lubing my shaft. Xe used it to coat xyr palm, stroking me faster.

I thrust my hips up, aching for some sort of relief.

Xe dragged the pinwheel down my body again, delivering another series of shocks.

"Damn it," I sighed.

"How does it feel?"

"Good," I gritted out. "Bad. Good. Terrible and wonderful?"

Moss chuckled. "All of the above?"

"All of the above."

The pinwheel ran over my skin, drawing a path across my abs and chest.

I closed my eyes. I wanted to revel in what was happening to me. I loved every second of it, even if the electricity hurt. It was almost too much, and somehow not nearly enough.

I bucked my hips, pumping hopelessly.

I was so desperate to come. Moss tightened xyr grip, creating a vice around my cock.

"I need to come," I rasped. "Please. I'm so close, Moss."

"Good boy," xe whispered. "Keep fucking my hand. Keep fucking my hand like a little slut."

"Fuck," I moaned. "Keep calling me a slut."

"Keep begging," xe growled.

Fuck. I huffed, thrusting harder. "*Please, please, please.*"

"Keep going."

There was a taunt in xyr tone, one that was driving me wild.

It was enough to nearly make me cum. My eyes fluttered as I strained against the cuffs. Sweat slicked my body as xe dragged the pinwheel over my skin.

I gasped from the zaps, everything intensifying.

Moss tightened xyr grip. "Harder, little *tarax*."

I'd lost track of how many times I'd come over the last 24 hours. It was unending.

This had to be the millionth one, and it was every bit as intense as the first. I cried out as I finally came, cum bursting from the tip of my cock. My fingertips dug into the bed as I finally found my crescendo of pleasure and relief.

"Good boy," Moss praised. "Look how much you came for me."

My eyes flew open as I panted, looking down at the mess I'd made. Xe brought xyr hand to xyr lips, tongue swiping over my cum and lapping it up.

"You taste so good," xe praised.

Xe cleaned off xyr hand, every drop of come disappearing. I licked my lips, basking in the rush of coming so hard.

Moss leaned down, brushing xyr lips over mine gently. I parted mine, hungry to taste xem. Our tongues met, xyr sharp teeth scraping over my bottom lip.

Xe drew back and slid off the bed. I pouted, which only made xem laugh as xe went back to the closet.

"What more could you possibly do to me?" I asked.

Xe gave me a look that told me how silly of a question that was. Xe had a closet full of BDSM equipment, xyr submissive tied down, and hours to fuck me.

"So, so much. Really, we have all day and night, don't we?"

I groaned and xe laughed. Even though I knew xe was planning to torture me more, I found myself smiling too. I laid my head back against the pillows as Moss returned with a glittering flogger with long strings.

"That looks..." I trailed off.

I recognized this toy from an ad I'd seen on a certain program a while back.

"Is that what I think it is?" I asked.

"Yes," xe said. "It is."

My mouth fell open.

This flogger was one of a kind, and one that had become very popular. Every strand was laced with microscopic needles that delivered a euphoric drug, one that was perfectly safe and intensified everything.

"We don't have to use it if you don't want to," Moss said. "I've never used it on anyone. It would be yours forever if we used it on you, since the needles would penetrate your skin."

"No, I want you to use it on me," I choked out. "Does it hurt?"

"I imagine so, but the drug supposedly turns that pain to a very intense pleasure. Which could be good or bad depending on what you like."

Moss knelt on the end of the bed, xyr tentacles writhing. I could see the slick oozing out of each one. Xyr muscles rippled as they drew the flogger back and then lightly splayed them over my stomach and chest.

I gasped, arching immediately. It wasn't the pain that was intense, because there was hardly any. It was the immediate euphoric flood that rushed through my body and mind. All of my nerves tingled as Moss dragged them down my body, even around my cock.

I huffed, panting and thrusting. I was powerless against its strength.

Moss flogged me again and then leaned down, sinking xyr teeth into my inner thigh. The pain flashed, sharp and poignant. I grit my teeth, yanking against the restraints to no avail.

Xyr tongue smoothed over the bite and xe drew back, holding my gaze. "More?"

"More," I rasped. "Again. Please."

Xe let out a short growl and bit me again, hard enough that I felt xyr teeth sinking into my flesh. Xe moaned against me, xyr tongue swiping over the wound.

Tears leaked from my eyes and I huffed, my cock straining. The pain and the pleasure—all of it was so much more intense. My vision swirled with the effects of the drugged flogger as Moss bit me again, inching further up my thighs.

More.

More.

More.

My thoughts became louder and I felt Moss there again, a strange echo through my mind that connected us. Xe could feel me, and I could feel xem. I could feel how much xe enjoyed the taste of my blood.

How much xe loved *ravaging* me.

Xe moved up, hovering over me as xe bit my hip.

"Mark me," I whimpered. "Mark me as yours. I want the whole world to see these bites tomorrow."

Xe snarled against me, fangs flashing as xe left more marks.

Every piercing bite made me cry, more tears falling, but the aftermath of the pain? It was delicious. It was fulfilling. It was satisfying beyond what I ever expected from myself.

I bucked against xem, my muscles burning as I yanked on the restraints.

Struggling felt good.

Being held down and bitten felt even better.

I gasped as Moss sank xyr teeth around my nipple. "Fuck," I moaned.

Xyr tongue swiped over, soothing and pleasuring me. Moss reached down between us, spreading xyr tentacles as I grew hard again. I moaned as xe sank down, spearing xyrself with my cock. I thrust up, filling xem as xe bit into me again.

"Oh gods," I rasped.

Xyr body was tight around me, squeezing and milking me as I pumped up and down slowly. Pleasure mixed with pain, creating an intoxicating concoction.

By the time xe made it to my lips, we were both panting and grunting. I kissed xem deeply as we kept grinding against each other. Moss planted xyr hands to either side of my head, xyr horns looming above me. I traced every line of xyr beautiful face with my gaze, the way xyr lips parted and eyes fluttered as xe took me.

"Good boy," Moss huffed. "I can't wait for you to fill me. I want to feel you come inside."

I moaned, kissing xem again as we kept moving together. The pleasure through our connection bloomed, growing more intense the longer we went on.

"I'm so close," I whispered.

"Fill me," Moss urged. "Come inside me."

We groaned together, my hips snapping harder and faster. With one more thrust, I came again, filling Moss with everything my body had left.

We melted against each other. Xe laid xyr head on my chest, listening to my heart pound. I closed my eyes, basking in the feelings shared between us.

"We'll rest," Moss whispered.

"And then do it *again*?" I asked.

"And then do it again."

CHAPTER 10
Nerves

MAX

"How are you feeling?"

Moss spooned me in bed, xyr arm draped over my waist. The sun was already rising again and I was realizing that our heat bliss was coming to an end.

"Good," I said softly. I cleared my throat, fighting back tears that sprang up out of nowhere.

Moss nuzzled me, pressing a kiss to my shoulder. I'd gotten enough sleep to make it through the rest of the day. But part of me wished I would have skipped the sleep and done more with Moss.

The pinwheel, the drugged flogger, the restraints, hours of sex. My body was satiated, exhausted, and yet it still yearned for more. More than that, it was the time spent with Moss.

I didn't want it to end.

"I need to get dressed," I sighed. "Are you working today, too?"

"I am. I have to check on the whole situation. Hopefully things have been resolved."

"I hope so," I said.

Silence settled between us but it was full of so much unsaid. Finally, I let out a long breath and turned over, cupping Moss' face.

"I don't want it to end. The heat was unlike anything I've ever experienced."

Moss pressed a gentle kiss to my lips and smiled. "I don't want it to either. But, I'm thankful for the time we had together. And I'm glad my initial grumpiness didn't scare you off."

I couldn't help but laugh. I leaned back, sighing as I splayed over the bed.

Moss sat up with a groan. "We have to get going. I'll drop you off at rehearsal, okay?"

I smiled. "Okay."

After two mind-blowing days full of sex with Moss, returning to the "real world" felt like a dream. After exploring all of the toys in Moss's closet, I'd learned that I loved pain a lot more than I'd believed before. And that I liked edging, even if it was a special sort of torture that drove me crazy.

But if it was coming from Moss? I was okay with going a little crazy.

We'd eaten breakfast together this morning and then xe had returned me to my hotel room, which was still a mess. The smug looks I'd gotten on my way back to the hotel room had me rolling my eyes. The entire troupe and crew knew where I'd been.

After Moss left for work, I'd made my way back down to the rehearsal space.

Now, I was standing in my dressing room, trying not to think about Moss. Trying not to think about how not only did I want to date xem...

I wanted more.

It was easy to envision a life with Moss, but that easiness ended once I started thinking about logistics. I was a burlesque dancer. I traveled the universe.

And Moss? Moss lived here.

It wouldn't be fair to ask xem to change xyr entire life for me, right?

Not being near xem made my skin itch. I was having a hard time not thinking about everything, which was why I'd been staring at my costumes for the last fifteen minutes.

Rehearsal was in about twenty minutes and my body felt nice and relaxed, despite the constant churn of uneasy thoughts.

I went over the costumes again, looking for any visual flaws or things I needed to mend. There was nothing wrong with any of them, but I couldn't choose which one to wear for tonight's show. I couldn't decide what performance I wanted to do. I could stick to my first one, but I was daring and wanted to go outside of the box.

But maybe Madam Moonie would tell me to hold back some.

"Damn it," I sighed.

All I could do was think about how crazy the heat had been. The connection between us had been so strong, strong enough that we could hear each other's thoughts. How wild was that? I was still in awe of everything.

I hadn't wanted it to end. Leaving this morning was far more difficult than I'd expected.

Our lighting team was still upset about the equipment issues, but Madam Moonie managed to soothe everyone for the most part, and I was certain Moss would handle everything.

I felt bad for not being an assistant at times. It was hard knowing she was juggling everything alone. Every time I tried to help, she swatted me away. I had to remind myself that she'd managed the Galactic Gems just fine before me.

And that I was a star now.

I scowled at the costumes. What the hell was I going to wear tonight? And why was it so hard to choose?

Which would Moss like most?

I heard a knock at the door and glanced up, not surprised to see Stella there. Her braids were wrapped up in dark purple silk and she wore a flowing black robe with a bodysuit beneath it. She always looked flawless.

She crossed her arms, giving me a *look*.

All I could do was sigh. "Don't look at me like that."

Stella snorted. "Oh god. Should I even ask? How's it going?"

She had that knowing smirk, the nosy one.

I raised a brow, trying not to laugh at her. She was clearly fishing about Moss. "Do you want to hear *everything*?" I teased.

"Maybe not, but I'm surprised xe's not hanging around with you right now. I mean, you've only been gone for two days and in the meantime, Zin and Toras kindly filled me in on Arborian 'heat' habits."

I blushed hard and didn't feel a lick of shame about it.

"You could have taken off longer, you know. Madam Moonie would have understood. I've heard that heats usually last longer than a couple days."

"I can't do that," I mumbled.

She was right though. Part of me wasn't convinced the heat

was completely over, especially since I couldn't think about anything else but Moss.

Being with Moss, fucking Moss, kissing Moss, being used by Moss.

Moss, Moss, Moss.

What in the hell is wrong with me?

I cleared my throat. "Besides, this is my first planet. My first time as a performer. I can't skip out on any shows. That would look bad."

"We would all understand. Especially given how sexy xe is."

I snorted, but she was right. Moss *was* sexy.

I wished that xe was here right now. It would only be a few hours before I saw xem again, which wasn't long even if it felt—very dramatically—like a million years from now.

We'd see each other again, right?

"I'm going crazy," I mumbled to myself.

That thought lingered with me. Xe told me xe'd contact me soon, and then left, and I realized that I hadn't given xem a way to. Although xe knew where I worked and was staying and...

"Hello? Earth to Max?" Stella teased. "You're thinking really hard about a lot, huh?"

"Xe had some things with work," I said finally. "I think there might have been some trouble with one of the employees when it comes to our equipment refund."

"Oh," she said with a frown. "Well, hopefully everything gets worked out. The equipment damages were not terrible, but still pretty extensive considering we didn't even go that far from point A to point B. But really, I think it was more that the person blew up at Madam Moonie. And she was calm, but the way he treated her was ridiculous. I don't know why, but he seems to hate humans."

Ugh. Great. If that were the case, some things would

make sense. "Moss agrees. And yeah, I'm not going to worry. I'm sure it'll all be fine and I'll see xem again and this was more than just some wild and deeply fulfilling two night stand."

"Whoa," Stella said, coming into the room. "Aw, Max. It'll be okay. I'm certain Moss feels the same way about you. How could xe not?"

I gave her a helpless look as she stopped next to me. "I really like xem," I whispered. "I mean, the sex was mind blowing. Amazing. But beyond that, I feel..."

"Empty without xem."

"Yeah," I sighed.

Stella pressed her lips together. "Did you mate with xem?"

"No," I said. "No, we didn't. Unless we did and I don't know."

"Oh, you'd know," she laughed. "So ask xem out?"

I gave her a withering look but she only snickered at me. Highlighter glimmered on her cheekbones, only adding to the sparkle of mischief she wore so well.

"Come on. Seriously? Just ask to see xem again. Make it happen."

"Maybe I like being seduced and asked out," I mumbled.

She rolled her eyes. "Well, at the very least, make sure xe has a front row ticket to see you shake your ass."

She had a point.

"Fuck me," I sighed. "I didn't even get xyr contact."

"Well... good thing Madam has it?"

"You bitch," I said dramatically.

"And Madam may have given it to me in case someone needs it."

"Stella," I hissed.

"You can thank me later," she teased as she handed me a piece of paper. "Such an old fashioned way, too. So, talk to me about your costumes. What are you wearing tonight? The same one as opening night?"

"Doing something different tonight," I said as I snatched the paper away. "Thoughts?"

I looked up at her. I always forgot how tall Stella was until we were standing next to each other. She put her hands on her hips, letting out a soft hum.

"Well," she said. "All of these are good options, but I think it would be fun if you wore a mask, especially...Okay hear me out."

I raised a brow.

"It's a little provocative..."

"We're burlesque dancers," I hissed. "Come on."

"Okay, but the mask over your privates. It has a *beak*."

We both stared at the jeweled mask that had a long, bird-like nose.

"Only that, though. Pasties, a mask, and a jockstrap."

"You mean going down to only a jeweled butt plug is too much?"

She burst out laughing. "I mean, I'm sure your lover would enjoy it."

Once again, I was blushing hard. The thought alone of xem watching me perform made me feel a whole new level of anxiety and excitement.

"What are you doing tonight?" I asked. "*Solar Strip?*"

"No, I'm changing it up to one of the others. I usually rotate through my main three and occasionally will come up with something new but...if it works, it works. You'll find the ones that work for you and then it'll be easy. Rehearsals are more for tech purposes at this point."

I breathed out, already running through everything in my head. "I think I have an idea for what I'm going to do."

"Try it out," she said. "Might as well, right?"

"You're a bad influence, you know."

She stuck her tongue out. "I'm the best and you know it. See you on stage, *Maximalist*."

She left me alone in the dressing room and I snorted. I rolled my shoulders, thinking over everything she'd said.

And the idea for the show...

I could run it. Might as well, right? Maybe rehearsal would get Moss off my mind for just a little bit.

Maybe.

CHAPTER 11
Pre Show Workout

MAX

Sweat dripped from my body as my song ended. I stood at the edge of the stage to an audience of other performers and tech crew, and received a few claps and whistles.

I breathed out slowly and then straightened, closing my eyes for a moment. That had been a damn workout, but one that would be worth it. I flexed my hands, stretching them after gripping the straps and holding myself in the air.

The performance would be amazing. Stella had been right about it being provocative.

I felt the high of trying something new as I grabbed my robe from the stage, sliding it over my body. I was basically naked except for the mask over my cock, jockstrap, pasties, and now robe.

But, it ran perfectly. There had been a couple spots I wanted to change some minor things to make it smoother, but I felt confident in running it for the show tonight.

I bounced off the stage and was surprised to see Moss waiting at the edge of the oasis, a smile lighting up xyr beautiful face. Even from this distance, I could feel xyr warmth.

My heart pounded as I stepped into one of the small boats and rowed myself across the serene waters. Moss stood there, the sun haloing xyr horns and long hair.

Xe was glorious. How had I ended up being with someone so damn gorgeous?

I was nervous, but happy to see xem.

"Hi," I breathed out as the boat came to the edge of the oasis.

Moss leaned over and tapped the helm. I was shocked to see a light flash, and the boat went still as if adhered to its place by invisible ropes. Xe held out xyr hand for me, helping me step onto solid ground.

"Hi," I said again like an idiot.

"Hello," xe teased. "How are you feeling?"

"Good. Out of breath. My hands might blister after this one, but it'll be worth it."

"Well, from what I saw, that was a very provocative performance." Xe grinned brighter. "I enjoyed it very much."

I preened under the compliment. "It was just the rehearsal," I said. "I'm not even in my makeup or glitter yet. I was going to call you, but..." *I was too damn scared too and worried about overstepping even if that's absurd.*

Moss surprised me by tugging me close to xem. Xe tipped up my chin.

"When I realized I'd left without giving you my communication contact, I couldn't focus all day. I worried you'd think I didn't want to talk," Moss said. "I hope you know I've been thinking about you for hours non stop."

I let out a pent up breath. "Really?"

Xe snorted and leaned down, kissing me in front of everyone. I heard a couple snickers, giggles, and whoops—along with the pressure of what *had* to be Madam Moonie's gaze on us.

"*NO FORNICATION IN PUBLIC!*" her voice echoed through the oasis.

Moss drew back with a coy smile.

"I was going to call you," I rushed out. "I got your contact from Stella who got it from Madam..."

"Take a deep breath," Moss said softly.

I did as xe asked, and felt myself starting to calm. "Do you want to come to the show tonight? First row?"

I hadn't felt this nervous in ages. Why was I so damn nervous?

"Yes. Does that mean I get to see you after?"

"You can see me any time," I teased, although I meant every single word so much that my stomach twisted.

"You can see me any time too," Moss murmured.

I found myself falling into xyr gaze. The hues of purples that reminded me of crushed amethyst. The way xyr horns stretched up, ending in fiery orange tips.

I took a deep breath and snapped myself out of the reverie, trying not to fall too far because then I'd trip over myself again.

"What do you do now that rehearsal is finished?" Moss asked. "Do you have anything else to do between now and the show?"

"No...I'm free for a couple hours. And then we'll have the show and I'll be working the rest of the night. And you'll get to see us all."

"I will," xe chuckled. "I won't interfere as much as I did the first night, I promise."

"Maybe I like it when you interfere," I mumbled. "How did work go? I know you mentioned there were some things..."

Moss winced. "Not as well as I hoped. The Galactic Gems have been sent a sum to cover the damages, so that is finished.

But the employee who had an issue has been a problem. He has a lot of hostility towards the situation. And towards me for not solving it the way he wanted it solved, which was kicking the troupe off our planet."

"We should tell Madam," I said.

"I have informed her," Moss said softly. Xe cupped my face, xyr touch gentle. "I'd never let anything bad happen to you or to your troupe. And I don't think security would let this person through now, especially since you have a prince floating around here."

True. That did help a lot. Ever since Zin started traveling with us, our security at shows increased by a significant amount.

Still, it made me nervous that someone could be so upset that Moss would feel the need to remind me xe would protect me. My stomach did a little flop.

"Why does he hate the troupe?" I asked.

"That, I don't know."

I pressed my lips together. I couldn't imagine why. An angry past customer, perhaps?

I turned around and waved at Madam, who was stationed about thirty feet away. She gave me a thumbs up, which was my signal that I was good to go until showtime.

I slipped my hand into Moss's and gave xem a tug. "Come on. Let's order some food and go to my room. I should take a *nap*, I think…"

"A nap?" Moss questioned as I led xem down the path that went back to the tree with our rooms.

A hotel tree? I didn't know what to call it.

I smirked, feeling frisky. "Yes. A *nap*."

Moss was clearly puzzled but didn't argue. I gathered that if xe had to go back to work, xe would have told me by now.

Within a few minutes, we were climbing the steps up to my hotel room. I practically shoved Moss inside.

"I'm starting to think you don't intend to nap."

"I certainly don't," I teased.

I watched the realization creep over xyr expression. "Are you still in heat, little *tarax*?" xe teased.

"Maybe?" I breathed out. "Didn't you say it could last longer?"

"I did."

I kicked the door behind me. I locked it and then pulled off my clothes, which wasn't much thankfully.

Moss raised a brow as I marched up to xem, pushing xem back onto the bed.

"For someone much smaller than me, you are mighty."

"Moss, I need to fuck you," I groaned. "I'm dying here."

Xyr expression turned to shock as I climbed on top of xem. I straddled xyr hips, letting out a low, desperate moan.

"I'm begging," I rasped.

"Oh and I like it when you beg," xe said, xyr voice turning dark.

In one swift motion, xe had me pinned beneath xem, xyr hand around my neck. Xe leaned down, tracing the shell of my ear with the tip of xyr tongue.

I bucked my hips against xem, moaning. I was so fucking hard. I wasn't sure what had come over me aside from the full, hot, lustful need that I needed to satiate.

"Grind against me," xe huffed. "Good boy."

I whimpered as I kept grinding, my fingers digging into the blankets. Moss let out a low growl, gripping my hair and holding me in place as xe thrust against me.

"Do you want to fuck me?" xe murmured.

"Please. Please, I need to be inside you."

"Are you sure that's what you want?"

"Please," I cried. "I'm so hard right now. All I've done since this morning is think about being with you again."

"Such a needy little slut," Moss teased.

"Yes, I fucking am."

Moss chuckled and flipped us over, moving my body with ease so I was back on top and straddling xem. I pushed back xyr robes, undoing them quickly until I exposed xyr tentacled cocks and hole. I spread the tentacles apart, seeing that xe was already wet.

"Fuck me," Moss said.

It was a command. It was a command and a release. I leaned in and wedged the head of my cock against them, gently easing forward. I moaned as I slid inside xem, my head falling back as pleasure rolled through my body. Xe was hot and tight, milking my cock with every inch.

Xyr tentacles wrapped around my balls, which had become one of my favorite parts of our intercourse. I moaned, thrusting fully forward, giving xem everything.

"Good," xe rasped. "Hard. Fast and hard before someone needs you."

I grunted, planting my hands on xyr hips as I started to fuck xem. I slammed into xem over and over, panting as I drove myself to the edge quickly. I was already so close to exploding, and I wasn't able to slow down.

Xyr tentacles tightened, massaging my balls. I cried out, fighting the urge to immediately come.

"Come, little *tarax*," Moss whispered. "Fill me up."

Fuck.

I pumped harder, my fingers digging into xem as I slid in and out. Finally, I came to the edge, unable to stop. With one final thrust, my voice echoed through the room as I came, filling xem with every single drop.

I collapsed on top, still catching my breath. My head was

spinning, my body buzzing with an electric current of satisfaction.

"We'll stay like this until you're ready to eat," Moss murmured gently, stroking my hair. "I love it when you come inside of me."

"I love it too," I rasped, smiling against xem.

Could this always be how my rehearsals went?

"I'm going to order you some food before you jump me again," Moss said.

"Sounds perfect."

CHAPTER 12
Show

MOSS

I made my way to the front row and took my seat between two other Arborians, both of which gave me a nod of respect, especially at the sight of the necklace I wore. I had changed into some of my silk robes that had golden details sewn into them. They were soft against my skin, making me feel good.

I glanced around, spotting a couple other officials on the council in the crowd. There was a soft chatter around, the anticipation already growing.

A Galactic Gems sign beamed in the sky with their show time and logo. I looked up, appreciating how it looked against the backdrop of trees and sky.

I was excited to see the entire show. I'd promised myself I'd sit through it all so that I didn't interfere with Max's work. As much as I wanted to always be by his side, I didn't want to annoy him.

After the work day I'd had, this was refreshing. Dealing

with Dio had been unpleasant, and the council had not taken his threats lightly. Especially towards me. I simply couldn't understand why the situation had escalated so, except that it seemed he did not like human beings.

I'd asked so many questions, but none of them had given me answers to any sort of real reason for his behavior.

The way he'd looked at me though...

I tried to shove those worries away.

The good news was that his case was out of my hands. I could move on, focus on my own tasks, and get to know Max. I wanted to know everything about him. In the few days we'd known each other, I'd already learned a lot, which pleased me.

What I didn't want to think about yet was how he would be gone in six weeks.

The thought of him leaving made my stomach twist. I didn't want to think about that, and kept shoving it out of my mind, refusing to acknowledge that a serious decision would likely need to be made.

I wanted to court him.

After the show tonight, I would ask him on a date. A real date. One at a place where we'd dine together. And perhaps I would get wine and invite him back home, where I could ravage him.

I shifted in my seat, swallowing hard. Once again I was thankful for the robes I wore and how they kept the world from seeing my tentacle cocks aching and throbbing at just the mere thought of touching him.

A spotlight flashed above, and a second came on, turning the oasis a brilliant aquamarine blue. The lights complimented the natural glow of our crystals.

My eyes swept to the stage at the center of the pool. The curtains were closed for now.

"Welcome to the Galactic Gems Burlesque Show!" Madam Moonie's voice echoed around us.

I had to admit, while that woman slightly terrified me, she was certainly a wonderful entertainer and leader.

"Tonight, we are here to *tease, titillate,* and *entertain.* Our gems are here to sparkle, enchant, and entice."

The crowd clapped and hollered, rowdier than the first night. I smiled, relaxing into the atmosphere, and joining in. The lights began to move, creating a rainbow across the stage in a circular motion. It was dazzling.

"Put your hands together for our first performer, the lustrous Lady Luun!"

The clapping continued as the curtains began to draw back.

A single spotlight hit the stage, highlighting a woman that was seated in the air on an apparatus that looked like a crescent moon. It gleamed the same way her glittered leotard did, the crystals beaming beneath the lights.

"Incredible," I whispered.

Every performer seemed to know how to put on a show.

The music started, a cinematic tune that swelled up. I closed my eyes for a moment, letting the music sink in. I could feel the vibrations, my ears twitching.

I opened my eyes as Lady Luun began to gracefully unfold from the crescent moon, spinning in the air as she moved. Her long brown hair fell in waves and she moved with the same practiced ease that I'd seen from all of the performers. I watched in amazement as she flipped upside down and then somehow folded her body up, climbing on top of the moon and balancing there in a very precarious way.

There was a collective gasp from the audience as she dropped down the same moment the music changed from cinematic to pop. She held onto the bottom of the lyra, her costume changing as she managed to strip off a piece.

Once again, I was amazed. Every Galactic Gem had their own talent, and they knew how to shine. I could understand why Max felt the pride that he did. Getting into this troupe had to be exceedingly difficult, but he'd done it.

Her performance ended a few minutes later and was followed by Stella Starz. I'd seen and heard Stella before and recognized her as she stepped onto the stage. Her voice was unforgettable. And I knew she was mated to the Lazulian prince I'd met, along with a Tourmalin chancellor.

Her song rose through the venue, echoing into the night sky. The stars glittered above as if clapping to her melody, cheering on the beauty of it. It was provocative and lovely, and left everyone in the crowd breathless, longing, and horny.

When her act ended, Madam Moonie's voice came on again. "Please welcome our next Galactic Gem! An aerialist, a performer, an eclectic rising star—give it up for *the Maximalist!*"

I clapped and cheered, my voice rising up.

The lights flashed and then dimmed, going dark. While I'd seen Max's performance earlier from afar, nothing had prepared me for how wonderful it would be with the music, costume, and lighting.

The music started as a spotlight lifted up into the air, revealing him there. He held onto a strap, a cape wrapped around his body, disguising everything beneath.

I felt a swell of pride and excitement as the crowd cheered for him.

He's mine. That was all I could think as I watched him. And how fucking wonderful he was.

How had I been so lucky to meet him?

I'd been alive for a long time and there had been many

moments where I had doubted fate. But seeing him on stage and how much of a star he was, all I could feel was lucky to have even breathed the same air as him.

He spun and the robe slipped down, revealing the pasties at his nipples.

Nipples I've played with.

I let out a soft hum, shifting in my seat again. I was mesmerized as he moved, his muscles rippling as he turned upside down and into a series of other positions.

I knew he was strong. But seeing him do things that defied my imagination entranced me. Every movement was practiced and measured. The way his muscles rippled as he defied gravity amazed me.

I grinned, clapping as the robe finally slipped all the way free, revealing nothing but the glittering mask over his cock.

It appeared like that was all he wore.

The crowd lost it as he came down to the stage, dancing and moving with the music.

Something caught his foot and he stumbled forward, his knees hitting the stage hard. No one else noticed though and he didn't miss a beat, even if I felt the echo of pain through our connection.

Fuck.

That meant it had hurt.

That also meant...

I blushed, heat creeping up my spine as I realized how deeply connected the two of us still were.

Typically once a heat finished, that connection disappeared unless it was finalized by a mating bond.

I bit my lower lip as I continued to watch him. He kept dancing and moving, thrusting his hips.

Even from this distance, I felt him looking at me. I smiled, clapping as the end of his performance neared. He came to the edge of the stage, grabbing onto the nose of the mask as the last beat hit, and the lights flipped off.

Everyone clapped and cheered. The roar of the crowd was deafening, full of energy and excitement. I leaned forward, squinting through the dark to watch him get off stage.

He was limping.

I couldn't stay put. I let out a low growl as Madam Moonie's voice came on again, but I couldn't hear her. I was already moving, standing and heading for the back of the venue. Within a couple of minutes, I was taking the back way towards their 'backstage' area.

Several security guards waited ahead. I drew out my identification as I came to them.

"I'm here to see Max," I said.

"Madam Moonie already cleared you," one of them grunted, stepping aside. "Figured you'd be on your way."

I nodded and rushed past them, my heart hammering. Max was okay, right? What if he wasn't? I'd felt the pain through the bond.

I saw Stella and rushed towards her. Her mates stood next to her, both of them appearing concerned.

"Is Max okay?" I asked.

"He'll be okay," she answered quickly. She reached out, placing a hand on my shoulder. "Breathe. We have injuries sometimes and we keep healing pods on standby. I'm shocked you even noticed, he concealed it well."

"I heard his bone crack," Zin muttered.

Terror washed through me.

Zin winced. "I'm sorry. I shouldn't have said that. He'll be out soon, I'm sure. Uh...This is our mate, Toras."

I gave the tall magenta tentacled Tourmalin a nod, but I was struggling to remain calm.

"I felt his pain," I said. "But he kept performing."

"Well, the show must go on," Stella sighed. "And Max is stubborn. And he knows how to take a fall. He's an aerialist, and from my understanding, a well practiced one."

"His mate will not accept that answer," Toras said very seriously.

Mate. I swallowed hard as all three of them looked at me, waiting for me to disagree.

But at the moment, I didn't.

I wished more than anything we were mated because then I'd be able to speak to him easier through our mental connection.

Another approached us and I recognized her as the first performer, Lady Luun. Her hair was drawn back in a bun and she'd changed out of her performance wear. "He'll be okay," she said. "He just twisted his knee and bruised the cap. He'll be out in a couple minutes. Also, hi."

I gave her a nod, my ears flicking as music rose through the venue again. I could hear the crowd laughing and cheering. I glanced up, even if my attention was still on waiting for Max.

"How many performers are there?" I asked.

"There are nine of us," Stella answered. "Myself, Lady Luun, Little Miss Mercury, the Maximalist, the Milky Maid, Betty Battlestar, Nebula Van Dazzle, Fiona Firefly, and Zodiac."

"Technically Madam Moonie is a performer too," Lady said with a grin. "Although her performances are like mythical creatures. Rarely seen and you have to be special to see her in person."

"I've seen videos," Stella said, giving Lady a smirk. "There's a reason she's our captain."

I was getting antsy. I was taller than everyone here, except for perhaps Zin, and looked over their heads as I waited for

Max. Within a couple of minutes, I spotted his bright orange hair and took off towards him.

His eyes lit up when he saw me. He held up his hands and started to speak, but I scooped him up, letting out a low growl.

"I'm okay," he breathed out. "Hey. I'm okay, I'm okay."

"I *felt* your pain," I growled.

He grabbed hold of my face, forcing me to look at him. He planted a kiss on my lips, and that soothed some of my immediate worries.

"You didn't have to leave the show," he said, pouting. "I'm okay. This happens sometimes. I tripped over my stupid robe. The healing pods patched me up."

I finally breathed out, feeling myself relax.

He kissed me again. "Put me down, though. Everyone is staring."

"I thought you liked being the star," I teased.

He snorted as I let him down. Before I could say another word, he grabbed my hand and led me towards the edge of the waters. We could just see the performer on stage, the music swelling.

"I wanted you to see the whole show," he sighed.

"I loved everything I did see," I told him. "Truly. Everyone here is so talented. And the things you can do with your body..."

Max looked up at me with a smirk. "You like what I can do with my body, huh?"

I blushed hard and shook my head, looking back towards the stage. He kept snickering, which only made me blush more.

"I'll remember this," I mumbled.

"I hope you do," he chuckled.

I swallowed hard, sliding my gaze over to him again. "Hey Max?"

My heart started to pound.

"Yes?"

"Will you…will you go on a date with me?"

He startled, looking up again. "A date?"

"Yes," I whispered. "A date."

Max grinned at me in a way that made me feel like he was the center of my entire universe. "Of course I'll go on a date with you."

GALACTIC GEMS

MOSS

CHAPTER 13
First Date

MOSS

I couldn't stop adjusting the robes I wore. I smoothed my hands down them once again, feeling a flash of nerves as I waited. The reservation was made and I was early to pick up Max.

Everything would be fine.

Right?

The heat had ended, but that didn't mean that I stopped constantly thinking about being with him. Last night, I went to the show and watched him perform. The energy had been something to witness, the crowd completely seduced and enamored, even with his injury–which had definitely made me overreact.

And all I could think about was how much he already meant to me.

I'd gone to sleep with him on my mind and then woken with him on my mind. Both of us had work to attend to today, and the hours had passed by slower than ever. I'd been counting down the minutes until I got to see him again.

Now, we had our first date. Maybe we'd done things backwards, but I didn't care. I was looking forward to spending time with him, courting him, and spoiling him.

Our first date.

I was most definitely overthinking things. It was hard not to. I had feelings for Max. There was no doubt about that. But, I felt like I had done things backwards. In my society, it was common for someone to go into heat immediately and then to court each other, and yet I worried that I hadn't done enough to earn Max's affection.

"I gotta say, you don't look well, friend."

I looked up, startled to see an alien that was as tall as me wearing nothing but a hat, boots, and pants that did not cover his backside. He offered me a tip of his hat, two of his four arms crossed over his chest.

"I'm just waiting," I said. "I have a date."

"Oh, you're the one who took off with Max. The gals have been giggling about the two of you."

The *gals*? His accent was unlike anything I'd ever heard outside of a movie. I wanted to ask him more questions, but I didn't have the chance to. Max came bounding out, wearing a glittering blue shirt and black high-waisted pants. He also wore a set of boots that made him a little taller.

Seeing him was a breath of fresh air. I smiled as he came up to me, enjoying the way that he beamed.

He's so cute.

"Are you ready?" I asked.

"Yes," he said. "More than you know."

That made me happy too. I glanced up at the alien again, giving him a slight nod before hooking my arm with Max's.

"Have fun."

"Bye, Raider," Max chuckled.

I raised a brow as I led Max away. Max let out a soft chuckle again, looking up at me.

"He's mated to Mari," he explained. "The two of them are on their honeymoon, but were stopping by to say hello. I missed performing on stage a little bit even though it hasn't even been that long."

"Would you miss it?" I asked. "Even if you were just on a little vacation?"

"Yes," he said wistfully. "I think I would always miss it. Being on stage is something that I've dreamed about my entire life, and I've finally been able to do it. And with the Galactic Gems. I've been dreaming about being in their troupe for years. I started as an intern. I got lucky considering what happened."

"What happened?" I asked.

Max made a noise, wincing. "It was a lot. The old assistant for Madam Moonie poisoned two performers. She tried to blame everything on me, using me to do tasks for her that I didn't realize were to make those things happen. That was when Stella had first met Zin and Toras, her mates. We got to the bottom of it, though, and after that situation, I became an assistant to Madam Moonie. And then after the last galaxy, she decided to give me a chance to be on stage. And now here I am."

I growled at the thought of someone framing him for such a crime. Especially knowing he would never do such a thing.

"You're a natural star," I said. "I don't know much about dance or the world of burlesque, but I know that I could watch you perform for hours and never be tired of it. I was enamored even on the first night."

Max blushed. "I didn't even think you were paying that close attention the night we met."

I scoffed. "How could I not?"

I let out a little laugh, thinking about it now. How cranky I'd been. Disgruntled that I had to go to a show to try to argue with a human about money. Little did I know, Max would change my entire world.

I was certain that he was my mate. Even after the heat, that much was clear. But I didn't want to pressure him into making a decision, especially now that his career was beginning.

What would it look like? I wasn't sure how the two of us could make it work. My life was very much rooted on this planet, and his was meant to be in the stars.

Could I leave it all behind?

It wasn't that my job was my life. It was just all I really knew.

A breeze lifted, sending ripples across the oasis waters. I raised my head up, soaking up the view of the massive trees that were my home. The crowns of leaves rustled, creating a soft sound that was so familiar.

Max slid his hand into mine, as best as he could anyway. My hand swamped his. He held onto me as I led him to the water's edge.

"Where are we going?" he asked.

"I made a reservation," I said. "There is a restaurant on the other side of the oasis. We will sail over to it, and enjoy our meal. I think that you'll like this place."

I held onto his hand, helping him into the boat. It rocked back-and-forth for a moment, and then I followed him, settling at the front. The moment we were both inside of it, it began to move to its own accord.

Maxed gasped, looking around. "The boat didn't work for us like this the other night," he said. "We had to have someone row."

I winced. Someone should have told them how the boats work. Although I wasn't sure it would work the same for humans, but for Arborians, the boats were in tune to our world and to our thoughts. It knew where I wanted to go, and therefore would take me there. Like the invisible paths that ran through the treetops, there were certain things on our planet that did not work for humans or even other beings. Our scientists believed it had to do with the crystals that surrounded the bases of our trees, while other people believe it was spiritual.

I explained that to Max, enjoying the way his expression changed from frustration to awe.

"Wow. That's amazing," he said. "We don't have anything like that on Earth."

I was curious about his planet. "What is it like? I've never been to Earth. Or your galaxy."

"It's...still recovering from a lot of past damage. Humans are very destructive. We didn't care for our planet the same way you care for yours. But, it's beautiful. I grew up in a small coastal city before we moved to one of the other planet settlements. I haven't been back in some time. Have you been to any other planets?"

"I've been to the ones in our own system," I said. "Several of the planets are just as stunning as ours, although they differ in many ways. Still, home is my favorite."

"I can see why," he agreed. "I've been to a few other planets and systems now, and this one has always been my favorite."

"Why is that?" I asked.

"There's something about it... It's magical. I don't know if it's the trees, the waters, the crystals, or the sky. But it calls to me. Maybe it's because of you."

My heart fluttered.

I felt the same way. I smiled as we drifted to the other side of the oasis. I leaned over the edge, staring down into the waters, and watching as fish swam by. His gaze followed mine, and he made a little sound of surprise.

"I didn't see these the other night either."

"They only appear during the day," I said. "They go down deep at night and stay away from the surface while it's dark. Their cycles are interesting."

Max smiled and then leaned back in his seat. He turned his gaze across the waters. The sun was setting soon, dipping us into a sort of twilight that I loved.

I felt my nerves rising up again and did my best to squash them. I hoped he liked the food at the restaurant. They did have a human menu, which I had double checked for, because I was worried he might not enjoy the cuisine.

The boat drifted to the edge, slowing as we landed. I carefully stood, balancing with ease and practice as I stepped out. I turned, holding out my hand to help Max. He wobbled for a moment, and ultimately, I decided to pick him up and lift him out of the boat. He blushed again, his cheeks turning dark pink.

I fought the urge to pinch them, amused by him.

Others around us gave us curious glances, and I knew that we had to be an odd pairing. It wasn't very often that a human ended up with one of us. Other aliens? Yes. But Max was special.

I led him towards the path that wound between several of the massive trees. It was a short and peaceful walk. The crystals were beginning to illuminate, casting their beautiful glow over everything as we made our way to the entrance at the base of one of the trees.

We were greeted by another Arborian. I waited patiently as they checked my name on the list, and then they led us through the restaurant. Others were seated at their tables, ones that were close to the floor. The scent of the food wafted through the air and my stomach growled.

Max made a small growl too. I glanced at him, and then realized it was his stomach as well.

"Hungry?" I asked.

"Very."

We were led to the opposite side of the restaurant to an opening outside. This was a large deck, one that hung over a cliff that hovered over another oasis. One of the largest in the forest, and really more of a lake. He sucked in a breath, his eyes widening as he stared out.

"This is amazing."

We took our seat beneath the branches, the peaceful sounds of leaves brushing against each other from the breeze making me feel at ease. Surrounded by all of the natural beauty, all I could do was focus on Max and how lovely he was. A stab of desire rolled through me and for a moment, I wished we had indulged our desires before coming to eat.

But, maybe we would save that for dessert.

He caught me staring at him and raised a brow, his lips tugging into a smirk.

"Anything to drink?" our waiter asked.

"Water for both of us, and I will have an *iothie*."

"Right away." They left the two of us alone.

"What is that? An *iothie*?" he asked.

"It's a mix of different algaes that are very good for my kind. It has a lot of energetic benefits, which I could use."

He wiggled his brows. "Energetic, huh?"

I winked at him as he leaned over, his hand slipping into mine on top of the table. The public display of affection turned me on. I caught other people staring at us, but I reveled in the attention. I loved the idea that his hand in mine meant people might think we were together, that he was mine.

"Thank you for taking me on a date," he whispered. "I hope you don't feel like you have to."

"And I hope you feel like you didn't have to come. I wanted this. I want to know you more. I know that the way we met was unconventional, but..." *I'm falling in love with you.*

I couldn't bring myself to say it out loud. I was falling in love with him. And I was worried about scaring him away. And along with that, I wanted to bend him over the table and claim him in front of the entire restaurant, just to show the whole world that he belonged to me. And that I belonged to him.

My tentacles stirred, and I sucked in a breath, urging my senses to relax.

"I like you," I finally whispered.

Max laced his fingers with mine. "I like you too. More than like you, considering everything that we've already done together. I have a question."

"Ask me anything," I said softly.

"How do Arborians mate? From what I've heard, usually it's from a bite for other aliens? But we have bit each other, and are not mated unless we are and I just didn't realize..."

Oh. I forced myself to take an easy breath, even as the nerves shot through me. Mostly because I wanted so badly to complete a mating ritual with him.

The thought of it alone made me hard.

"It's not just about sharing a bite," I said. "To be mated to one of us, and for us to be mated to someone else, there is a ritual of sorts that tie us together on a different level."

"Like our souls?"

He sounded very doubtful. I understood his doubts, even if I did not have them myself.

"Yes," I said.

"How does it work?"

I was about to answer him, but then the waiter came back. He sat our drinks down and gave us an expectant smile, waiting for us to order.

Max winced. "I haven't looked at the menu yet," he said. "But I'd like to try your food, not the human menu."

"May I order for you then?" I asked.

He nodded quickly. For a moment, I got lost in his eyes, and nearly forgot where we were. The waiter cleared his throat, waiting patiently.

I rattled off several menu items, some of which were my favorites and others that I hoped Max would enjoy too. The waiter nodded and left us alone again, the two of us letting out a nervous laugh.

What was it about going on a first date with someone that was so nerve-racking? I knew that he liked me. I knew that he wanted to be with me. Both of us knew that we had compatibility, and yet...

My stomach couldn't stop flipping back and forth. My heart couldn't stop hammering in my chest.

"The ritual is very intimate," I whispered. I leaned forward, keeping my voice low. "First, we start by ingesting a sort of medicinal plant. It changes your headspace and can make you see things. And then you mate, then you share your mating bite, and then you simply accept each other as mates. Once you do so, truly do so, something happens. I don't know how to explain it, other than something changes on a quantum level that perhaps we still don't understand. Our scientists have tried to figure it out many times, as have others from other planets. But, no one knows. I just know that's how it's done, and that's how it's always been done. It's very sexual, very private, very intimate."

"Sounds very lovely." He stroked the top of my hand with his thumb, letting out a soft hum.

"I..." I almost asked him if he wanted to do it. But instead, I bit my tongue, looking away from him as I blushed. Heat crept down the back of my neck and down my spine.

"Moss."

There was so much longing in his voice. I refused to look at him, not able to. Because if I did, everything would be so clear. Even if we didn't always understand each other's expressions, it would be so painfully clear that I was in love with him already.

"Moss, if you want this, we can talk about it."

I felt a pinch of pain. Because it wasn't that I didn't want to talk about it. It's that I wanted him to want it too.

"I don't want to make you feel like you have to do anything," I said. "Fate or no fate."

He scowled. "I don't feel like I have to—"

And of course, the waiter interrupted us again. I fought the urge to snarl, holding myself together as he placed our food on the table. It was a full spread of different vegetables and delights from our planet. The scent made my stomach growl again, and I reached for my drink, taking a large sip.

I could feel the replenishment through my system immediately, and realized that in my heat, I had forgotten to eat. That was fairly common, our bodies could hold nutrients for a very long time. But I definitely felt the hunger now.

"Enjoy," the waiter said.

"Gods, this smells delicious," Max said.

Whatever had happened between us just now had passed, the two of us now entirely focused on the food before us.

"I should've asked if you have any allergies," I said.

"I don't," he said giddily.

He took a plate and started piling different types of food onto it. I couldn't help but chuckle as I watched him. He was mixing things that definitely did not go together, however, I was not going to correct him. He would figure it out.

I did the same with my plate, piling it high. I took a small saucer and filled it with a sauce. I took a pair of utensils and dipped the first bite of food into it.

He paused to watch me, paying attention to how I did things. I did everything slowly, feeling a sense of warmth as he copied me.

"These are braised mushrooms from the Horned Valley," I explained. "They've been seasoned in a sauce for several cycles, and then cooked on an open flame. They pair best with the sauce, at least in my opinion."

I took a bite, letting out a soft sigh of enjoyment.

Max did the same, and his eyes widened with pure delight.

"It doesn't taste like a mushroom," he said. "I mean, I've had mushrooms. And this is...this is so much different. I don't know what to compare it to."

"It's one of my favorites." I picked up another piece of food, a lime green disc with a flaky edge. "I don't know what to compare it to for you, but we call it *stome* and it comes from the stamen of a plant from a different region of the planet."

I dipped it into the sauce again and ate it. It was crunchy and flaky and slightly sweet.

He took a bite too, and made a face and he chewed.

"No?" I chuckled.

"It tastes like butter," he said. "Which was not expected. But it's good too."

I grinned. I've never sat down at a meal with someone who had never tried our food before, but it gave me a different sort of enjoyment getting his reactions.

"One day, we'll do this with earth foods," he teased.

"I won't eat meat, though."

"Believe me, there are plenty of other things."

The two of us continued to eat, trying different items until both of us were so full we could barely move. The waiter came back and cleared plates, packing everything into a container for me.

"I've heard about Arborian wines," Max said.

"We can stop and get a bottle if you want," I offered.

"Can I come home with you tonight?"

Home.

I nodded. "Please."

I wanted him. Desperately, hungrily. The idea of us working off our full meal together pleased me.

I stood up and held out my hand for him. "Wine, home, and..."

"Bed," he said with a smirk.

"*Bed*, indeed."

CHAPTER 14
Upside Down

MAX

Moss smirked as xe uncorked the artisan bottle of wine. The bottle itself should have been in a museum. It looked like a mix of crystals and blown glass, truly stunning.

"Am I just going to drink it while you carry me?" I teased.

"Yes. Why not? Open your mouth."

I smiled as I opened my mouth for xem. Moss stepped closer and tipped the bottle slightly, giving me just a taste.

Arborian wine was in a league of its own. My brows shot up as the flavors burst over my tongue. It wasn't too sweet and was perfectly balanced, not that I knew anything about wine. Not really.

"Wow," I said. "This is glorious."

Xe chuckled and handed me the entire bottle. "And potent."

Moss turned around and lowered xyrself expectantly. I glanced around, blushing as a couple of other people passing by gave us strange looks. I didn't care though. I climbed onto xyr back and held onto the bottle, taking another sip with a snicker.

Moss carried me down a path and then scaled a tree, drawing a squeak from me by how fast xe moved. I held on for dear life as xe came to a massive branch, walking down it and then across a path I couldn't see.

I was starting to get used to feeling like Moss was magical. And it was wonderful.

I held onto xem as I looked out over the massive trees and the crystals below. The glow splashed over the roots, creating an illuminated tangle at the base of the forest.

This was my favorite planet. Of that, I was certain. I'd never get over how beautiful it was. It was truly otherworldly.

Moss crossed another invisible path with a chuckle. "Doing okay back there?"

"Yes," I said. "More than okay. I'm enjoying the view."

"I take it for granted now, I fear," Moss sighed. "But I like hearing you talk about it. What's your favorite thing?"

"Probably the invisible paths," I said, staring down. My stomach did a nervous flip right as Moss stepped onto a branch. "I can't even see them, but it feels like you're a wizard."

"Perhaps I am," Moss teased.

"The wine is delicious," I said, sipping more.

"Our wines are lovely, I have to admit. Save some for me."

I agreed and then fought the urge to ask Moss about our conversations earlier. Our date had been perfect, but the food had interrupted what felt like a pretty important conversation.

I took another sip of wine as Moss came to the entrance of xyr home. The door slid open and xe stepped inside.

And froze.

My stomach dropped as I took in the destruction.

Moss's home was completely turned upside down. Items

were strewn across the floor, furniture broken. Moss let out a low growl and let me off xyr back.

"Stay here," xe demanded.

"What?" I hissed.

Before I could get another word in, Moss moved in a blur. I always forgot how fast xe was until moments like this. My mouth fell open as xe disappeared. I heard a shout and my stomach flipped as I took off after xem.

I came to Moss's destroyed office where the window was open. Moss was leaning against it, xyr shoulders stiff.

"They escaped," he said.

"Who would have done this?" I asked, looking around, horrified. "Who was it?"

Moss didn't answer.

Everything was destroyed.

"Moss," I whispered, looking around. "We need to call someone. I'm so sorry."

Moss let out a frustrated breath and turned around, xyr shoulders sinking as they took in the mess. "I'm sorry, Max. I'm going to have to attend to some things. I wanted us to enjoy the rest of the evening, but this is horrifying."

"It is. Can I stay with you?"

Xe was quiet for a moment and then nodded. "Yes. Please."

I nodded, trying to keep my temper at bay because I wanted to punch whoever had hurt Moss this way. The thought of someone breaking in and destroying everything enraged me.

I followed Moss back to the living room where xe pulled up xyr communications system and started a call.

Xe was speaking so fast, I was unable to understand everything xe said, my communication piece struggling to keep up. Within a few minutes, several official looking Arborians arrived.

Moss crossed over to me as the others inspected xyr home. "They'll be here for a while," xe sighed. "Are you okay?"

"*I'm* fine," I said. "Are you? I'm angry that someone did this to you. Do you know who?"

"I suspect that it was Dio," Moss said. "Given that he sent me a lot of angry messages and today he was reprimanded at work. I think this is a sort of retaliation."

I winced. That meant that all of this had started just because of some damaged equipment.

"Don't make that face, little *tarax*," Moss said gently. "This isn't your fault. I'll handle this and then we won't have to worry about anything else."

I nodded, although I remained unconvinced. I was worried about something else happening. I didn't know Dio or why they were taking everything so personally, but clearly something was there.

All I could do was hope that the authorities found him and kept him from doing this sort of thing again.

Moss tipped my face up, planting a gentle kiss on my lips. "I'm going to take you back home."

But this is my home too.

The thought was like a sharp little blade. This wasn't my home, but it was xyrs, and I didn't want them to be alone.

"I want to stay," I breathed out.

"I don't know how long they'll be around."

"I don't care. I want to stay with you," I said.

Xe was quiet for a moment and then nodded, kissing me again. "Okay. If you're sure."

I nodded, very sure. Moss turned as one of the officials called xem over. I sighed as xe went, chewing on my bottom lip, watching them talk. Occasionally, one of them would study me, but they never asked me anything.

After an hour or so, I found a couple of glasses that weren't broken. I poured each of us a full glass of wine as the last of the officials left. Moss locked the front door and sighed, xyr shoulders deflating.

"Come have wine," I said. "Come have a moment. And then we can start cleaning up."

Moss turned and looked around, xyr eyes flashing with a mix of anger, sadness, and strength. I could tell xe was doing everything xe could to hold it together.

Xe crossed through the mess and came around the counter to me, sliding xyr arms around me. I leaned against xem and closed my eyes.

"I wish there was more I could do," I whispered.

Moss snorted. "You are doing far more for me than you might realize. I'm going to hold you for some time."

"As long as you want," I whispered. I turned in xyr grip, wrapping my arms around xyr waist and pressed my face to xyr chest.

I didn't count the seconds or minutes. Instead, I just stood there, being held and holding xem too.

I want this forever.

I couldn't bring myself to say that though. I couldn't bring myself to tell Moss just how much I wanted xem to come with me while I was performing. Between tours, we could come back here, right?

My lips pressed together and I tried not to think about the future or how in just a few weeks, I would be leaving this place.

And potentially Moss too.

Moss kissed the top of my head and then released me. "Wine and..."

"Cleaning up as much as we can," I said. "And then maybe we can do something more enjoyable."

"Always such a thirsty boy," Moss teased.

"Always," I said as I reached for my wine. I took a sip and groaned. It really was some of the best I'd ever had.

"The council has agreed to repay me for the damages, and as far as Dio, he's being searched for," Moss sighed. Xe picked up xyr glass and took a sip, letting out a soft hum. "He won't get very far. Our world might be large and we might not be as *modern* as other places, but he will not escape for very long."

"What will happen then?"

"He'll be charged with breaking and entering. He wasn't very smart about how he did this. His fingerprints are over everything..." Moss swallowed hard. "I am concerned because he doesn't seem to care about himself. And that makes him more dangerous."

"We can talk to Madam," I said. "Increase security."

"Yes."

"I can't help but wonder why he hates humans so much," I said. "Or maybe it's just burlesque performers? Or maybe it's just us."

"I don't know," Moss sighed. "I cannot imagine hating humans just because, but there are some aliens that don't like how connected all of our worlds have become. If he's one of them, then that could very much be it. And then how I supported humans over him..."

I nodded, thinking about it.

"We can't assume everything though. I'm leaving everything else to the others. My main goal is to keep you and the rest of the troupe safe from anything else."

"I hate that this happened to you," I whispered.

"Me too. But I would rather it happen to me than you."

I took a deep breath, trying to calm myself. I didn't agree, but I understood what xe meant. If we were in opposite positions, I'd say the same thing.

"Let's start cleaning up," I said. "We'll get everything as organized as possible."

"We still have a bed at least," Moss mumbled.

"That's all we really need, right?"

Moss smiled despite everything. "I think so, huh?"

I leaned up and kissed xem, lingering there for a moment before looking back at the living room.

I pushed up my sleeves. "Let's get started."

CHAPTER 15
Comfort

MOSS

Max and I groaned as we lowered ourselves into the hot water. Steam drifted around us, our muscles exhausted for reasons I wished were more exciting than cleaning up the mess Dio made.

"At least he didn't fuck up the bathroom too bad," I mumbled, glancing around.

This room had mostly been spared. For that, I could be thankful.

Max nodded as he sank down. "Agreed."

My office and living room had taken the brunt of Dio's wrath.

"Try to put it out of your mind," Max reminded me softly.

It was hard to do.

I should have realized that once Max put his mind to something, he was determined to get it done. The sun would be rising soon, but my home was clean and somewhat empty given that we'd gotten rid of everything broken. We'd gathered a lot into bags, disposed of them, and repeated the process over and over. Every shard of glass, every snapped piece of furniture—all of it was gone.

It felt like I'd just moved in.

It hurt. It hurt more than I could admit, but I kept reminding myself that it was just items.

It was all replaceable.

Max, however, was not. And neither were the rest of the Galactic Gems. I was worried about them. Worried about everything. I couldn't stand the thought of someone being hurt because of this.

I'd been trying to understand Dio's motives. For hours, I'd tried to put myself in his shoes, to understand where I'd gone wrong. But ultimately, it felt like he'd done this out of pure spite or hatred, and I couldn't figure out if it was more than him simply hating the performers for whatever reason.

"You have that look again," Max whispered.

I swallowed hard. "I can't put everything out of my mind."

"It's been hours, my love, and nothing else can change for now. I don't think either one of us will figure this guy out."

"Agreed," I sighed.

I pressed my lips together, letting the heat permeate through me.

"I want to hold you," I murmured.

Max nodded, already moving.

"Come to me," I said.

He waded across the pool to me, sliding his arms around my waist as I pulled him into my lap. I rested my chin on his shoulder and closed my eyes, breathing in his comforting scent.

Maybe I could put things out of my mind if he were with me. It was easier to focus on Max.

"It's going to be okay," he said. "We can talk to Madam later today. I'm sure she'll be concerned, but she'll know what to do. This isn't the first emergency any of us have dealt with."

"You need sleep first," I reminded him.

"I need to be with you," he countered.

I swallowed hard and nodded. I leaned back against the side of the pool, admiring him, feeling him. I could stay like this forever, simply basking in his presence and enjoying the feeling of not being alone.

What was I going to do when he was gone?

The thought was just another knife piercing me.

Max ran his hands over my chest, oblivious to the way my own thoughts and feelings were tearing me up inside. I wanted him so badly. Forever and always.

His lips brushed mine gently, but I needed more. I wanted more. I deepened it, our tongues rolling together. He moaned and rocked his hips, grinding against me.

"I need you," I panted.

"I'm yours," he said. "All yours."

A low growl left me as I kissed down his body. He still had marks from where I'd bitten him. I kissed them now, making my way down to his nipples. I swirled my tongue, listening to his breath hitch and moans slip out.

I loved it when he made those sounds.

He reached down between us, gripping my top tentacle and stroking. His head fell back as he groaned, his body shivering against me.

"Max," I rasped.

He lifted himself up, already knowing what I needed. I gripped his ass cheeks, parting them as my tentacles worked together, writhing against him before slowly pushing in.

We gasped together as he sank down.

"Too much?" I asked.

"No," he groaned.

My fingertips dug into his hips as I held him in place, his body stretching around me. I kissed the base of his throat, feeling his pulse against my lips.

"Oh gods," he grunted, planting his palms on my shoulders. "Bite me."

The heat between us grew, full of lust and potent desire. I bared my fangs, scraping their sharp tips against his fragile skin. He moaned as he started to move his body, rocking back and forth.

My tentacles moved inside of him as I sank my teeth into the base of his throat. He screamed, the deep cry ending on the softest of moans.

"I'm not going to last long," I rasped. His blood wet my lips, the metallic taste making me hunger for more.

Pollinay. Mate.

I wanted to mate with him completely, to tie our souls together forever.

I groaned against him, thrusting my hips up as he rode me. The water sloshed around us and I grabbed onto him, lifting and turning. I bent him over the edge of the pool and thrust in deeper.

"Fuck," he whimpered. "Harder."

I dragged my nails down his back, leaving long red streaks. He let out a gasp, pushing his ass back against me as he took me. My tentacles throbbed inside of him, writhing as I pumped in and out.

I leaned over him, reaching around and gripping his cock. I stroked him as I took him, fucking him harder than I had before.

My lips skated over his shoulders, leaving butterfly kisses, lingering as I continued to pleasure him. I was already close to the edge, and I was holding on, forcing myself not to come yet.

I wanted to last as long as I possibly could.

Mate. Mate. Mate. It kept coursing through my mind. I couldn't stop thinking about it with him, thinking about completing the ritual. I wanted to be connected to him on a deeper level. On a level that I couldn't possibly understand, but I craved so desperately.

I kept fighting myself on it. Every time I had these thoughts, I tamed them.

What would happen if I stopped fighting myself?

Max whimpered, his muscles rippling. After the nightmare that had turned into this night, being with him felt like the best sort of dream. One I never wanted to end.

"Oh gods," he groaned.

With one more thrust, I couldn't stop myself any longer. I gasped as I came, my head tilting back as I filled him. I felt him come too, his seed dripping over my hand in spurts.

I brought my hand to my mouth, licking up every drop. The taste of him sat on my tongue as I leaned back, breathing in his erotic scent. He was breathing hard, his pants filling the room. I stroked his back, and then gently eased out of him.

Before he could go anywhere, I wrapped my arms around his hips and lifted him out of the pool, putting him on all fours where his ass was facing me. He gasped as I leaned forward, sinking my tongue inside of him.

I could taste myself inside of him, and that turned me on. I ran my tongue around the rim of his ass, feasting on him. I moaned, pushing my tongue deeper into him. My seed dripped out, filling my mouth.

"Fuck," he grunted. "That feels so good."

I plunged deeper, closing my eyes as I ate him out. When the last of my come was gone I pulled back, licking my lips.

Max turned around and I pulled him back into the hot water. He wrapped his arms around me, holding me close as we floated towards the center, both of us coming down from the high of coming so hard.

I could feel him getting more and more tired. He needed to sleep soon.

"I'll grab the soaps," I said.

I got out of the pool for a moment, grabbed our soap, and then returned. Within a few minutes, the two of us were scrubbed down and clean, and ready to get into bed. We dried off and made our way towards the bedroom, now which mostly just consisted of the bed itself.

Max practically dove for his side, flopping down with a grin. He patted the blankets beside him and I got in next to him, pulling them around us.

"Will you sleep?" he whispered.

"I'll nap," I murmured. "Tonight was a lot. I appreciate you more than I can express for staying with me and helping me get things together and for being with me."

"Of course," Max said. "We'll get through this and once they catch Dio, it'll all be fine."

He wasn't wrong. Once they caught him, everything on that front would hopefully go back to normal. But the only thing was, the longer we spent together, the closer we got to Max leaving.

The closer we got to him being gone from the galaxy at least until they came back the next time. And I wasn't sure that I could wait that long to see him again.

What if he didn't even want to see me again?

I wasn't sure where all of the insecurities were coming from. Maybe it was because I hadn't been in a relationship in a long time, or maybe it was because this one already meant so much to me. But I had all these doubts plaguing me.

I wasn't sure if I was good enough. I wasn't sure if Max would even want to stay with me.

After what happened tonight, part of me wanted to just leave this place. Everything was gone, and it would be easier to start over. Right?

Would I travel the galaxies with Max? Would he even want me to? Would Madam Moonie let me join their spaceship? I had all of these questions, and unless I spoke them out loud, I would never get the answer. But the idea of asking scared me. The idea of making him feel like he had to be with me didn't feel right.

"You have a look on your face again," he whispered sleepily. He let out a soft yawn, his eyes starting to drift shut. "Whatever you're thinking about, I promise you it'll be okay."

"But you don't know what I'm thinking about," I chuckled.

He smirked and gave a dramatic shrug. "Maybe I do. Maybe I can read minds."

"You're very silly and very cute when you've been thoroughly fucked and are sleepy."

His smirk turned to a broad grin. "Mhmm. Goodnight."

"Goodnight," I purred.

He could always fall asleep so fast. I shook my head as he drifted off, a soft snore following. What would he dream about? Would he think about me? Human dreams had always fascinated me to think about, since Arborians were not the same. It would take me longer to fall asleep, especially as I mentally worked through everything that had happened again.

I couldn't help but wonder what would have happened if Max and I had been here.

I swallowed hard, tracing his face with my gaze. His long lashes, his bright hair, golden skin. Sometimes I found humans so strange to look at, but so beautiful in their strangeness.

The night had been hard, but Max had stayed with me through every moment of it. He'd comforted me. And he'd kept me from falling apart.

I smiled and closed my eyes, trying to focus on resting, if only for an hour or so. It wasn't quite time for my rest yet, but it wouldn't hurt to nap some.

Falling asleep next to someone I was falling in love with just felt right.

CHAPTER 16
Break In

MAX

A few days passed without anything else happening except that the more I knew Moss, the more I loved xem. The only lingering problem was that Dio had yet to be found, which put all of us on edge.

I wiped the sweat off my forehead with a cloth as I stepped onto one of the boats. I'd just run another rehearsal, determined not to fuck up tonight like I had last time. Not only did I not want to be injured again, I didn't want to worry anyone.

I didn't want to worry Moss.

The boat hit the crystalized edge of the oasis. I hopped out and headed towards Madam Moonie. She stood on a platform, her attention on the stage as she directed everything. A pink earpiece glittered in her ear, allowing her to communicate with whomever she needed to.

"How was that?" I asked.

"Perfect," she said, offering me a wry smile. "I'm shocked you're alone today."

I blushed as she gestured to a chair next to her. I took it, settling in as the next performance started.

"I had a vision, you know," she said, giving me a knowing look. "Should have known a flash of orange meant you."

I chuckled. "Probably. I didn't expect this."

"I can't say I did either. Are the two of you official yet? Do I need to put you in a bigger cabin on the ship?"

I hesitated, feeling my stomach clench. "I don't know yet."

She raised a brow and then held up a finger, rattling a list of commands off through her comm piece. She cleared her throat and then turned her attention back on me.

"Talk to me about it. I assumed the two of you had already made the bond or whatever."

"We haven't yet," I said. "I want to. But I don't want to cross any boundaries with Moss and it's still so new. It feels crazy to just jump off the edge even if it feels right."

"Seems to be working for everyone else," Madam chuckled. She took a seat next to me, leaning back in the chair with a heavy sigh. "I can't let you go though."

"I won't leave," I said. "This is my dream. Joining this troupe is one of the best things to ever happen to me. I can't just walk away from this."

"I know. And Moss knows too, I'm sure."

"Xe does," I sighed.

And yet we hadn't talked about it in depth. Every time one of us brought anything up that existed past the date of my departure, the conversation immediately turned to something else. It was like neither one of us could bear to speak about it, but we had to at some point.

The last few days were amazing. We'd fallen into a routine

of each of us working and then getting together after. Staying the night, enjoying food, learning about each other. Our likes and dislikes. Our hopes and dreams, our hobbies and favorite colors, and everything else that made me love xem already.

"You need to talk to xem," Madam said. "Instead of dragging this out. Clear communication is hot. And so is establishing boundaries, especially if your future is a long distance relationship or not one at all."

My heart skipped a beat.

It was hard to imagine a world now without Moss by my side. Even a long distance one sounded miserable, especially when that distance spanned galaxies.

"It's..."

"I don't want to hear it," she said. "Don't tell me it's complicated or it's hard or you don't want to scare xem off because you know that's bullshit, Max. I've known you long enough. And I also know how fiery you can be. Don't be afraid to go after what you want. You've already come this far."

It *was* complicated, though. And scary. And I did worry that maybe I was building this up in my mind as something more than it was. What if Moss didn't feel the same?

"Alright," I sighed. "I'll talk to xem. But not until after the show tonight."

"Good," she said. "Now go get some rest. I'm sure you've been losing sleep."

Her smirk had me rolling my eyes, but she wasn't wrong.

"Is there anything you need help with?" I asked.

"Nope. Go get some rest and get a good meal in. I want you at your best tonight."

"Will do," I said as I got up, pulling one of my capes around me so I wasn't just walking around mostly naked.

I gave her one more friendly wave and then headed towards

the hotel tree. A gentle breeze swept up, ruffling my hair and the leaves above. Within a few minutes, I made it to my room.

I hummed to myself as I stepped inside and tossed my clothes down. I needed a hot shower and would have food delivered so I didn't need to get out until later.

Shower pics for Moss...

I smirked to myself and headed to the adjoining bathroom. I pressed my hand to the wall and the automatic system came on. The hotel rooms were nice and more modern. I found myself missing Moss's apartment when I was here though.

"Turn on the shower," I commanded.

The shower started and I adjusted the water temperature before grabbing my device and opening the camera. I stepped under the water and groaned as the hot water ran over my muscles, washing away the sweat and grime.

I was ready for the performance tonight. And I was ready to see Moss after a long work day.

Teasing xem would bring me a lot of joy. I took a picture of myself, angling the camera down so Moss would just barely see my cock. I sent xem the photo, followed by one more.

Moss: You little slut. What am I going to do with you?

I chuckled and shot back a sassy message.

Me: I don't know. What are you going to do? You're at work so you can't get to me ;)

I could almost feel Moss growl from here. I chuckled as I sat my device down and soaped up, washing off quickly as I kept hearing messages come through.

I snatched up the device again and blushed, squeaking as a video call came through. I hesitantly pressed answer, shocked to see that Moss was sitting in what appeared to be an office.

"You're at work," I hissed.

"And you're taunting me. Show me your cock, little *tarax*."

"Fuck," I mumbled.

I aimed the camera down, now fully hard and turned on. Moss let out a low growl. I shivered, the anticipation of seeing xem in person later growing.

"Stroke yourself."

"What if you get caught?" I huffed.

"Stop worrying about me and stroke yourself."

I grunted and planted my forearm on the shower wall, bracing myself as I held the device, showing Moss everything I was doing to myself. My cock throbbed in my grip and I moaned, stroking myself for xem.

"Good boy," xe growled.

I moaned, thrusting forward as I kept going. I closed my eyes, focusing on the pleasure rolling through me.

"*Keep going.*"

Xyr words only turned me on more and more. Being on camera apparently turned me on too, hotter than I could have imagined.

I was already close to coming but then a noise echoed through the bathroom.

Crash.

My head whipped up and I stopped, my heart jumping in my chest.

"What is it?" Moss asked.

"I don't know," I whispered. "Be quiet."

I could hear movement in my room. My heart pounded faster as I slipped out of the shower, grabbing a towel and pulling it around myself. I kept the camera turned on, but Moss had gone silent.

I inched towards the door, listening intently as I reached for the lock. The sound of crashing and things breaking followed. I pressed my palm to the lock button, activating it as silently as I could. I stilled as the movement came towards the door, pausing there.

Heavy breathing. A low growl. My eyes closed and I sent up a silent prayer that they'd leave.

Fear rolled through me. I didn't have any weapons. I didn't want to call out. I was stuck there, ice freezing my veins, my muscles stiff.

The doorknob slowly twisted, and the door jerked, but didn't budge. It shook violently for a moment, a growl coming from the other side of the door before the movement retreated.

My knees weakened. I waited until I heard nothing, no movement, no sounds, no rustling.

"I'm opening the door," I whispered.

"Just stay there," Moss said. "I'm almost at your hotel. Don't open the door."

"Okay," I said. "How close are you?"

"*Close.*"

I pressed my back to the door and sank to the floor, still shaking. What the fuck was that? Was that Dio on the other side? Why would someone break into my hotel room?

I drew in a steady breath and closed my eyes, trying to keep my temper at bay. The fact was—I wasn't strong enough to fight an Arborian.

"Max, I'm here."

Moss's voice echoed through the room. I jumped to my feet and unlocked the bathroom door, poking my head out.

"Fuck," I whispered.

The room was destroyed. Moss stood at the doorway, xyr expression the same as it had been the night xyr apartment was destroyed. Furniture was broken, and some of my stray costume pieces were ripped. Xe crossed over to me quickly and scooped me up.

"I'm taking you away," xe said.

"Wait, hold on," I said, pushing against xem.

"No," Moss growled.

"Moss," I snapped. "Put me down!"

Moss froze and then immediately put me down, hurt flashing across xyr face. "I have to keep you safe."

"I'm okay," I said. "But I'm naked. I'm naked and I have a show tonight, I can't just leave. We need to approach this logically."

"I can't think straight," Moss snarled, stepping closer. "What if you hadn't called me? What if he'd gotten in and harmed you? I would never forgive myself. Ever."

"That didn't happen," I said, curling my hand into xyr robes. I was still trembling, my heart rate through the roof. "I need to breathe for a second."

Xe swallowed hard and then closed xyr eyes, giving a subtle nod. "I'm sorry. I'm not trying to control you, but I can't handle you being in danger. I feared I wouldn't get here in time."

"You got here," I whispered. "You got here, and whoever it was destroyed the room but they didn't manage to break into the bathroom. They left."

"It was Dio," Moss snarled.

"I didn't see him," I said. "But I think you're right. I don't know who else it would be."

"I think you shouldn't perform tonight."

I immediately shook my head. That wasn't happening. Dio was not going to stop me from having my moment.

"Max," Moss pleaded.

"No. I'm performing tonight. This is my job, Moss. And more than that, it's my life. It's the most important thing to me. More important than anything else."

I shouldn't have explained it that way. The hurt I saw flash across Moss's face stung me too.

"I didn't mean more important than you..." I trailed off, my throat feeling closed up.

"It's fine," Moss said coolly. "What matters most right now is making sure you're safe. I'll find clothes for you to change into."

Before I could say anything else, xe pulled back and looked around the room, trudging through the mess until xe found something for me to wear.

I bit my lower lip, trying to find the words. Trying to figure out what to say.

Fuck. Why were things feeling so messy? I pulled the towel tighter around me as Moss came back to me, handing me a shirt, pants, and boxers.

"I'll be right here, but I'm going to call Madam Moonie and more officials. Go get dressed."

I swallowed hard and went back to the bathroom.

I just needed to communicate better. I needed to be honest about what I wanted with Moss. It was eating me up that we hadn't talked about our future in depth yet, especially given that we both seemed to want more.

And I needed this fucking monster to be found so he could stop interrupting our lives.

I finished getting dressed and stepped back out into the bedroom. I wasn't surprised to see that Madam Moonie was already outside the doorway talking to Moss. She glanced over at me and gestured for me to join her. I pulled on a pair of boots and then waded through the mess to them.

I didn't like the look on her face.

"You're off the show tonight," she said. "And before you argue, you know that it's the safest thing until this person is found."

"No," I said. I felt my cheeks flush. I looked at Moss, glaring at xem. "Did you ask her to take me off?"

Moss was silent, but winced.

"Max, xe is right about this. You were just attacked. What if something happened while you were on stage? That's the least we can do to protect you for right now."

"This is my life," I growled, stomping my foot. "This is what I do. I'm a burlesque performer. I can't just stop my life for this situation."

"You're a burlesque performer while you're alive," she countered. "I understand that you are upset, but your space was literally just violated. This person is dangerous. I'm sorry, Max. This will pass and you'll be back on stage in no time. And if you can't do it for yourself, do it for the other performers."

"They could still be in danger," I whispered. "This Dio guy seems to not like any of us."

"It seems that he has focused on you and Moss. Clearly. I'm sorry, but this decision is final. This is my troupe. I care about you, Max. I won't risk your life for a five minute performance."

I stared at her, biting back tears. It hurt more than anything else could have.

"I need a minute," I said.

"Max," Moss whispered hoarsely.

"Go away," I growled, turning from xem.

"Let him have a moment," Madam sighed. "And let's get this taken care of."

I stalked off and went down the stairs to the bottom floor, my head pounding. I didn't want to cry in front of my boss, especially over something that was arguably stupid.

I was angry Moss had asked her to take me off.

My shoulders rolled back as I came to a giant tree root. I climbed on top of it and sat, looking out at the oasis. Everything was falling apart and what the fuck was I supposed to do?

I was being childish. I was overreacting. But I didn't know how to explain how fucking important being a dancer was to me. The idea of missing out on tonight made me feel like Dio had won.

Which only made things worse.

I took a deep breath, calming myself. Finally, now that I could breathe easy, I thought about Moss. I was a complete ass to xem and xe was just trying to protect me.

With a groan, I leaned back against the root and stared up at the sky. I needed to get up and apologize. I needed to pull myself together.

Missing one show wasn't the end of the world.

"Fuck," I sighed.

I was an idiot.

I sat back up and slid off the root, the bark rough against my back. I walked back to the hotel entrance and climbed back up the steps to the second floor.

"Moss," I called. "I'm sorry I was an ass."

I rounded the corner and stopped as I came towards my room.

"Moss? Madam?"

They weren't here. I scowled and stepped into the room.

"Moss?" I called again, feeling panic creep through me for the second time today. "Where are you?"

Xe wasn't here. I rushed to the bathroom and checked, then checked the closet, before stepping back out of the room.

Where had xe gone?

"*Moss!*" I shouted.

The tears sprang again, but out of the fear that xe was gone. And Madam Moonie?

"Fuck," I rasped.

I took off down the steps and rushed out, screaming their names out into the open. My voice echoed, rippling through the trees with no answer.

They wouldn't have just left.

I took off running for the backstage area, moving as fast as I could. I needed help. I needed to find the others and we had to spread out.

What if they get hurt?

I couldn't think about that right now.

All I could do was get help, and all of us would have to go from there.

CHAPTER 17
Drowning

MOSS

Dio kept Madam Moonie and I walking, two weapons pressed to our lower backs. Every time I glanced at her, she looked absolutely pissed.

We'd been ambushed.

The moment that Max left, Madam Moonie and I had continued talking. But then, Dio appeared with two knives, and managed to surprise us.

The blades were dangerous enough that neither one of us argued. I ran through a plan again, trying to figure out the best way to escape him.

I wasn't sure we could out run him.

And with him having knives…

I wasn't sure we could overpower him without risking our lives.

We have to do something.

Negotiating didn't seem to work, but I decided to try again.

"Dio, we can discuss this. Whatever you want, we can discuss it. We both just want to be safe."

"Shut up," he snarled.

He shoved me towards the base of a tree that was not too far from the oasis. I'd been mapping the path we'd taken, making sure I'd be able to get back if the opportunity presented itself.

The blade pressed into the small of my back, cutting through the robes I wore with ease. One wrong move, and one of us could seriously get hurt. Especially Madam, given that she was human.

I stole a glance at her again. Her cheeks were bright red, her eyes shining with rage. Her lavender colored hair was braided down her back, her dress shimmering as she walked.

If looks could kill, Dio would for sure have been dead by now.

She slid her gaze over to mine as we walked, holding it for a moment.

Somehow, we would get out of this.

Dio guided us through an opening at the roots of a tree. I glanced around, trying to see if there was anyone nearby. Anyone we could alert. The hall was cool and empty, though, and he shoved us towards a closed door.

"Open it," he said.

I pressed my lips together and opened it. He moved quickly, shoving us inside.

I stumbled forward and swung my arm out, keeping Madam from falling too. She straightened herself, her expression pinching into further anger.

This place was a mess. He'd clearly been staying here for a few days. It was dark and smelled nauseating. I couldn't help but wonder how in the hell he'd avoided any of the officers though.

I needed to reason with him somehow. I wasn't sure how. I'd been unable to get through to him before today and it certainly seemed like I had no chance now.

At least he had taken me instead of Max.

Max.

I felt a sharp pain, but it wasn't from the blade. I felt bad for how I'd handled everything. I couldn't just barge in and demand things from Max the way I had.

And now we were in this fucking situation.

I turned my head slightly, looking as Dio started to turn to lock the door. Madam Moonie caught my gaze and nodded.

The two of us moved fast. I grabbed his wrist and shoved him back against the door, twisting as hard as I could. One of the knives dropped but he brought the other one up, piercing my arm.

I cried out, but I didn't release him, even as the pain made my knees weaken.

I grabbed him by the robes and we fell back, rolling on the floor. Madam Moonie dove for the other knife as he pinned me down, ripping the blade from my arm and holding it to my neck. She stepped behind Dio, pressing the point to his back.

I froze, breathing hard. The pain in my arm was excruciating. Blood dripped out, pooling around me.

"One more move and xe dies," Dio snarled.

Well, at least he got my pronouns right before murdering me.

Madam Moonie gripped the knife, her eyes blazing with rage. "I will kill you if you kill xem. Why are you doing this? What do you want?"

Dio growled, but he didn't move. "You humans ruin everything. Because of you I'm going to lose my job and—"

"I wouldn't have fired you if you hadn't acted the way you

did," I growled. "You blew up at someone for something that should have been easy to handle."

Dio let out a soft, crazed laugh.

"I remember you now," Madam Moonie said.

Dio went still, his eyes widening. I swallowed hard as he pressed the blade closer.

"You were someone who tried to touch one of my performers and I got you banned in a different galaxy. Like five earth years ago," she growled. "Dio isn't your name, is it?"

"It is here," he snarled.

"You stupid son of a bitch," Madam Moonie muttered. "Yeah, I remember full well now. So your problem is with me then."

My heart hammered, my vision dotting as the pain became almost unbearable. I had to hold it together though. I couldn't leave Madam alone with him.

"It's with both of you," he growled. "You took her side. You're an Arborian like me, and yet you sided with *humans*. And now you're going to be mated to one?"

"That's none of your fucking business," I snapped.

"It really isn't," Madam agreed. "It's kind of pathetic actually. Why don't you fight me, huh? I'm the one that kicked you out so long ago. It all started with me, not anyone else."

Her ferocity stunned me. Dio's eyes widened with rage, holding my gaze for a moment before it looked like he was about to turn for her.

If he did, I had to use what little energy I had left to grab this blade.

I grit my teeth as the pain made me want to scream.

Look at her. Look at her. Give me some sort of opening.

"What? Are you scared to fight a human?"

The moment Dio started to whip around, I snatched his wrist again and yanked. Madam Moonie lunged the same moment he did, thrusting the blade through his back shoulder blade.

He yelped, falling to the side. I kicked, sending him rolling as Madam held out her hand.

"You can't pull me up," I said.

"You'd be shocked by how strong I am."

She was right. She grabbed my hand and pulled, helping me to my feet. I didn't have a moment to ask her how in the hell she had become so unnaturally strong before Dio was fighting to get up, blood dripping to the floor.

"Run," I rasped.

She unlocked the door quickly and threw it open, dragging me with her. The two of us took off, although he was now right behind us.

Madam sprinted like a gazelle. My adrenaline kicked in as I followed, both of us heading back towards the rehearsal area.

"I'm going to kill you!"

Madam was getting further and further ahead. My vision was growing darker the more I moved, the blood loss becoming too much. I broke through an opening, spotting the oasis and a flash of orange.

Max.

Dio tackled me, the two of us hitting the ground hard. I heard a shout and scream as we rolled, my back hitting the sharp crystals that curtained the edge of the oasis.

More pain split through me. I gasped right as we rolled into the waters, plunging into the cool depths.

I felt Dio shove another blade into my ribs. I gasped, swallowing water and choking.

I saw hands grabbing Dio, hauling him back. I sank further and further, my body unable to move.

The pain was too much.

Max. I'm so sorry.

I couldn't breathe. I couldn't move.

Hands grabbed me, small but mighty. I felt them tugging at me and forced my eyes open.

Max.

His face wavered in front of me.

You're not going to fucking die, his voice echoed through my head. *Fight! HELP ME!*

How could I?

He struggled against me. Using the last of my energy, I tried to push up towards the surface, but it wasn't enough. I saw a flash of dark blue and magenta right as my vision went dark.

CHAPTER 18
Pulse

MAX

I grabbed onto Moss's cloak, tugging xem as hard as I could. I made the mistake of breathing in water, choking on it as I fought to pull xem back to the surface.

We were sinking further and further.

My nose and lungs burned. A set of tentacles suddenly wrapped around me as a blue figure swam past.

Zin and Toras.

The tentacles were already pulling me up. I tried to keep hold of Moss, but Toras pulled my hand away as Zin grabbed onto xem.

Blood clouded the water. We broke the surface and I coughed, trying to drag in air as Toras pulled me to the rocky edge.

"Cough it up," he growled, hitting my back. "You can't breathe water."

"Moss," I croaked.

Toras pushed me onto the rocky beach and then retreated to help Zin. Together, they pulled Moss out of the oasis. Several guards waited on the edge apprehensively for Zin, but he waved them off with a snarl.

"Go get help," he snapped. They dispersed quickly.

I crawled onto the rocky ground and coughed up more water, breathing hard as I cleared everything out.

"We've got xem," Zin called. "Xe isn't breathing."

Fuck. Fuck. Fuck.

"Oh gods. Max!" Stella landed beside me and patted my upper back, helping me spit up the rest of the water.

I'd nearly drowned trying to get xem out. I let out a choked sob, looking over at xem. Xyr skin was pale, xyr body unmoving.

"We need to get to a healing pod," Toras said firmly. "Raider!" he shouted.

I didn't look up to see where the cowboy alien was. All I could hear were Dio's shouts echoed in the background as some of the Arborian officers dragged him away.

"Flip xem over," Zin said.

He and Toras flipped Moss over. Zin wrapped his arm around xem, holding xem up slightly as xe hit xyr back.

"We need a medic!" Stella shouted.

There had been many times I'd been grateful for the range her voice had, and now was another one. Birds scattered above as people moved toward us.

Some of the water in Moss's lungs came gushing out. Panic flooded me as I sat there and watched, frozen as everyone worked together. Toras and Zin lifted Moss quickly, and then Raider rushed towards our group, joining in with all four hands.

"We got this," Raider said quickly. "We'll get xem to the pod."

"Move fast," Toras said.

Mari ran up behind them, coming to me and Stella with wide eyes.

"I think Max is in shock," Stella said.

"We've got you," Mari said to me, rubbing my back. "Xe will be okay. Moss is strong."

I couldn't move. I felt like I couldn't breathe.

The two of them pulled me up and led me behind Moss and their partners. We kept a healing pod on standby for stage injuries, and it was in one of the hotel rooms, which wasn't too far. But every second that passed, I felt like things were looking worse and worse.

"Over here!" I heard Madam Moonie call.

"Max," Stella said. "Are you okay? Do you need healing too?"

"No," I croaked.

I didn't need anything except for Moss to be okay.

I couldn't stop replaying the moment I'd seen xyr eyes close. Panic rolled through me again, fresh and strong. My pace picked up as we crossed to the tree where the pod room was, luckily on the bottom floor. We all followed Madam Moonie in.

"Get xem in," she said. "It'll work. It has to."

Her determination was keeping me from completely falling apart.

It was a silver machine that was large enough to host any alien or human. The three of them lifted Moss and placed xem quickly inside of it. Zin pressed a button and the cover slid shut, exhaling air as it started its process.

Madam Moonie pressed a couple of buttons and then we all stood back, waiting to see what would happen.

Please work. Please, please, please.

I needed Moss to be okay. The last thing I'd said to xem was awful. Tears streamed down my cheeks. I hadn't meant it. I didn't want xem to go away. I wanted xem to be with me forever.

Please, please, please.

I loved xem. I loved xem so fucking much and I should have told xem.

Madam Moonie looked over at me, her eyes darkening. She left the machine and pulled me into a hug, holding me close.

"I'm sorry, Max. I didn't recognize Dio at first but he is someone I banned from shows a few years ago because he attempted to touch a performer. I fear this is my fault."

"It's not your fault," I whispered.

She held me for a moment longer. "It'll be okay. Moss is strong. We got out of that situation because of xem."

I nodded, swallowing hard. She released me and I went up to the machine, listening to the sounds of the whirring and buzzing.

I'd yet to hear Moss's pulse be calibrated.

"I need to be alone with xem," I whispered.

"Max..." Stella trailed off.

"Please."

Everyone was quiet as they left, and I could feel their worries. But I just needed to be alone.

Madam Moonie lingered for a moment. "I'm going to call some of the other officials. Moss will be okay."

"I haven't heard a pulse yet."

The machine continued to whir and buzz as Madam slipped away. I continued to stare down at xyr face.

I despised myself right now. Why had I stalked off? Maybe if I had stayed, the three of us could have overpowered Dio.

I loved xem. I loved xem so much. I wanted us to have a future together, even if it meant taking some time to figure out what that would mean to us.

The thought of losing xem...

The thought of not having xem in my life...

I let out a choked sob, wiping away the tears. I needed xem to be okay.

Beep.

I sucked in a breath and held it.

Beep. Beep. Beep.

Xyr pulse.

My knees weakened and I sank to the floor, letting out a soft cry. Xe was alive. Xe was going to be okay.

"Max."

I looked up, not surprised to see Stella there holding a towel.

"We need to get you into something dry. Madam Moonie is handling the Arborian officers. Is xe..."

"Xe's okay," I rasped. "Xe has a pulse. The machine is working."

Stella blew out a breath, her relief immediate. She came into the room and sat on the floor next to me, wrapping the towel around me.

"Thanks for being my friend," I mumbled, laying my head on her shoulder.

"Of course. I'm so glad xe is okay."

I swallowed hard. "Me too."

What happened had been one of the worst things that I had ever experienced.

After I realized Madam Moonie and Moss were gone, I made my way to the oasis where I found everyone. We alerted the officials, and then everyone had started to try and figure out where they possibly could've gone.

Meanwhile, minute after minute passed. Minute after minute that Moss and Madam could have died. The only reason I hadn't completely fallen apart was because of Stella.

I've never felt fear like that before. And then when I saw

them run through the oasis, bursting through the trees, I had hope.

But then I'd watched Dio tackle Moss into the oasis and all of the *blood*.

I couldn't get all of the blood out of my head.

Diving into the water and trying my best to get to xem, pushing through clouds of red to reach xem.

I breathed out, pulling the towel closer around myself.

The machine made more sounds—promising noises that meant my mate was going to be healed.

My mate. Moss was my mate. I had been so certain before, but I'd been too scared to confirm it or say anything. But now that was all I could think about.

All I could think about was how it could've been too late.

I was lucky. They were both lucky.

Stella stayed with me, not talking or asking me questions, but just waiting there. Eventually, Madam Moonie came to the doorway, her expression pinched. "I'm sorry, Max. But they need to ask a couple questions. Can you step out for a moment?"

"I'm not leaving," I said. "I'm not leaving Moss until xe is better. They can send someone in or wait."

"I'll handle it," Madam said and then slipped back out of the room. I could hear her voice getting heated outside of the room and saw an official poke their head in, look at me, look at the machine, and then backing off and disappearing.

Beep. Beep. Beep.
Beep. Beep. Beep.

I closed my eyes, listening to xyr pulse over and over.

"Do you want me to stay with you? Or should I find some food and water for Moss when xe wakes up? Xe'll need xyr strength."

"That would be wonderful," I said.

Stella nodded and got up. "I'll be back soon, okay?"

"Okay."

She left me alone with Moss. I drew in a steady breath, staring at the wall as I waited and listened. How long would this take? Would everything be okay?

I went through everything over and over until I finally stood up, turning around to look down. Moss appeared to be sleeping and all of the vitals appeared to be good.

"Max."

I turned to see Madam with another Arborian.

"This is Dr. Otany. She's here to check on Moss and make sure the machine is working."

I nodded and stepped aside as she came in. She immediately started changing some of the settings on the machine with a soft hum. She had long pink hair that was braided back and wore magenta robes that were lined with gold.

"Xe will be okay," she said. "Getting Moss to the pod was the best thing you could have done. We'll still need to check xem at the hospital, though. Xe lost a lot of blood and while this can repair wounds, it cannot replenish blood."

"Okay," I whispered.

"I'll make a call and we'll get xem moved. Are you xyr mate?"

"Yes," I said. "Well, yes."

She offered me a soft smile and nodded. "Okay. Just hold tight. You can come with us. Does Moss have any other family who needs to be alerted?"

I hesitated. I wasn't even sure. My stomach did a slow flip, and I became all the more determined to prove to Moss that I was meant to be with xem when xe woke up. Which would start with learning if xe had family or not.

"Just me for now," I said.

We still had much to learn about each other, and I hoped we would have all the time in the world to do so.

"Okay. I will return in just a few moments. Stay here."

She left quickly. Madam Moonie came to my side and handed me a set of dry clothes.

"Get changed," she said. "If you catch a cold after all of this, I'll never forgive myself."

"I'll get changed, but also because I don't want to worry Moss when xe wakes up. Are you okay? You were taken too."

"I'm okay," she said firmly. "I've been in stickier situations."

I raised a brow. It was rare that Madam Moonie talked about herself, and I couldn't help but wonder what kind of life she'd led before the Galactic Gems.

She smirked. "That's all I'm going to say. Don't even think about prying. I'll come to the hospital after the show."

I'd forgotten all about the show. It didn't seem near as important to me now. "Okay. Break a leg."

The show must always go on.

CHAPTER 19
For Eons

MOSS

My eyes opened and I let out a long groan. Immediately, my vision was swamped by bright orange and the strange face I'd come to love more than anything else.

"Max," I breathed out.

His lips met mine and I felt his tears against my face. I kissed him hard, desperation rolling through me as everything came back to me.

Dio, Madam Moonie, us running and then me falling into the oasis.

I'd been so certain that would be it.

Max sniffled as he drew back. "I've never been so scared. I'm so sorry."

"Why are you sorry?" I croaked. "My love, this isn't your fault."

"The last thing I said to you was to go away. And I thought you were going to die. I am such an idiot. I've never been so scared to lose someone before. I love you. I love you—"

I reached up and cupped his face, silencing him. He was braced on the side of the hospital bed, his eyes red from crying.

"I love you," I whispered. "I love you so much. You have come to mean everything to me, even if we still have so much to know of each other. Even if you tell me to go away, I love you too much to leave. You're mine, little *tarax*."

More tears wet his cheeks and I thumbed them away gently.

"How are you feeling?" he whispered.

My entire body ached, but it wasn't anything more than that. I looked down at myself, realizing that the only thing covering me was a hospital gown. "I'm okay," I said. "I feel a little achy but otherwise, I am fine. How long have I been out?"

"Two days."

Two days.

Fuck.

I examined Max again, seeing how exhausted he was. He looked like he'd hardly slept or eaten.

"Baby," I murmured. I moved to the side of the bed, making room for him. "Come here. I am fine, you can hug me and be with me."

He sniffled as he climbed in. His arms slid around me and I tugged him close, pressing my nose to his hair and breathing in his scent.

"Have you been here the whole time?" I asked.

"Yes."

"And Dio?"

"I don't think we have to ever worry about him again. One of the officials did interview me at one point, but since then, I haven't heard anything. Everyone has been coming by to check on you."

"And you," I chuckled. "Please tell me someone has kept you fed."

"Stella has," he snorted. "Why are you worrying about me? You're the one who was stabbed twice and nearly died."

"Yes, well, I've clearly been in a healing pod and been given nutrients whereas you've been sitting here for days watching me."

Max looked up at me. "I'd watch you for years. For eons. Forever."

"And I'll love you for years, eons, forever."

He took a sharp breath and then melted against me.

"Go to sleep," I whispered. "I'm here now."

He tried to hold out for some time, but it wasn't long before his soft snores made me smile. I continued to hold him, thankful that fate had brought us together.

The hospital refused to check me out for another couple days. By the time Max and I made it back home, I was so ready to be in my own bed.

My body was fine, healed from all of the things that had happened.

From what we had heard, Dio was locked up and would not be a problem for any of us ever again. Destruction of property, kidnapping, and attempted murder were not things Arborians took lightly. We might have been a peaceful planet, but that only went so far.

The shows for the Galactic Gems had gone well, even though Max had missed another one. It didn't matter how many times I told him to go, he'd opted to stay with me.

Madam Moonie had stopped by more than once to check on us. I never got the chance to ask her how she had become so strong, or so fast, but I decided to let her keep her secrets and not pry.

It was really none of my business anyways, was it?

Max locked the door behind us, putting his hands on his hips. I raised a brow at him and smirked.

We'd discussed a lot in our time at the hospital, starting with what we wanted to do with our future. I had decided that my life was with him, and that I would leave here, and find work out in the other galaxies while I traveled with him and the rest of the troupe.

It felt right. It felt exciting. After everything that had happened, I wasn't against the idea of leaving here for a while. Especially if it meant, I got to see my mate shake his ass in front of many different crowds.

Mate.

"Are you ready?" I whispered.

Max swallowed hard, but then nodded. Both of us were more than ready for this.

I took a step closer to him, and then another, and then finally one more. I reached out, gently cupping his face.

The moment I touched him, the tension snapped.

I yanked him close as he lunged for me, our mouths meeting and a fervent kiss. I needed to be inside of him. I needed to feel his body around mine as I bit him and tied our souls together forever.

I broke for a moment, drawing the herbs out of my pocket. I'd crushed them down into a powder and added water, putting them into a vial we could share.

"That's the drug?" he asked.

"It is. Are you certain you want this? That you want me?"

"I love you," Max said. "I want to be your pollinay. I'm certain this is what I want. Are you?"

"More than certain."

I uncapped the vial and Max parted his lips for me. I poured half into his mouth and the rest into mine, swallowing.

The taste was sweet and earthy, but not bad. I blinked as Max let out a soft laugh, his eyes widening.

"That fast?" I rasped.

It hit me hard. Lust, need, a burning thirst to devour Max in every way possible.

"Oh," I rasped.

Max let out a low growl and practically threw himself at me. I laughed as he pulled at my robes. I leaned down, kissing him as I pulled his clothing off too. Within moments, our clothes were piled on the floor and we were both naked.

I scooped him up and carried him to our bedroom, plopping him down in the center of the bed.

"I need you now," he rasped, reaching down to stroke his hard cock. "Now and forever."

My heart swelled with pride. After everything the two of us had gone through, we'd risen above it. Both of us had things that we wanted to work on, and together, we would.

I love him. I love him so much.

My head spun as I climbed onto the bed. He pulled his legs back, ready for me to take him. I leaned down, kissing up his body. I ran my fingers over his skin, shuddering at how soft it felt. I wanted to worship him. I wanted this moment to be one that neither one of us forgot.

I could feel the connection already for me. Like we had felt during the heat, our minds were open to each other. His feelings flowed through me, the raw need that coursed in his veins.

"Mine," I moaned as my tentacles pressed against his hole. "Mine forever, little *tarax*."

My tentacles were lubed and ready to fill him. The tips rimmed his hole, readying him for me. He moaned and writhed, his cheeks flushed as I thrust forward, gently filling him.

I could feel the drug's full effect now. I felt like I was looking down at an angel, his body glowing. I could see the connection between us as he took my cocks, our gasps mirroring each other.

I felt it the moment we fully accepted each other.

It was as if there was a silent click, a wink from the universe, a kiss from the stars and fate.

"Wow," he rasped.

All I could do was nod in agreement. I couldn't think of a better word. *Wow* certainly seemed to capture the awe I felt the moment Max became my mate.

Mate. Pollinay.

Pleasure burst through me, but I took things slow. I wanted to savor every moment with him.

I planted my hands to either side of his head, looking down at him in reverie. He smiled, his hands sliding up my chest to cup my jaw. We moaned together as I pushed deeper inside of him, my tentacles writhing within.

Mine.

I'm yours, he answered.

My eyes widened in surprise and he chuckled, wrapping his arms around me and legs around my waist.

I felt the fervent need now. I grunted as I drove into him hard, pumping in and out. He groaned, his cock hard against me as we moved together.

I was claiming him.

I growled, driving harder.

Claiming my mate.

Our instincts took over, blending together as I leaned down and sank my teeth into his shoulder. He whimpered and then groaned, doing the same to my opposite side shoulder. His teeth tore into me, the primal action only solidifying our bond.

Everything was how it was meant to be. The taste of his blood wet my mouth and I licked my lips, moaning as pleasure bloomed between us. He grunted, his eyes fluttering closed as he got closer and closer to the edge.

Our mating ritual was almost complete.

"Fill me," he rasped. "Come inside of me. I'm there."

I was too. With one final pump, I came hard, filling him. I felt his hot cum splash against me too, our orgasms winding together.

I closed my eyes, basking in the pleasure and glow of us. Max kissed my neck, letting out a soft hum.

We were officially mates.

CHAPTER 20
Six Weeks Later

MAX

The ship landed slowly, all of the warning announcements echoing through the halls and our room. Moss let out a low grumble, raising xyr head.

"You can go back to sleep," I whispered. I got up and hit the mute button so the announcements would stop echoing and disrupting our sleep.

Xe nodded and sank back down into the blankets, a soft snore following. I grinned and stretched for a moment, crossing our bedroom to a window that gave me a peek at our new destination.

Star City was the exact opposite of the Hörne Forests. Instead of massive trees that towered, it was a city of buildings that were made of white opal stone, glimmering obelisks all housed under a dome that protected it. This planet had lost its protective layers long ago, and now had alien-made ones. The dark sky glittered above, and while it was night, it was clear even from this distance that the city was very much alive.

While it was beautiful, I already ached for the beauty of Arbor. But, before we knew it, we would be back. Once we toured through all of the galaxies, our troupe would take a cycle off and Moss and I would return home.

I went back to bed and climbed in next to Moss. Xe let out a little growl, xyr arm snaking around me and tugging me close. I snorted. Moss did not sleep as much as me, but when xe did, xe was a grump if disturbed. It was the only time I ever saw xem be prickly for no reason.

"I can practically hear your mind," Moss mumbled.

"Someone is grumpy," I teased. "Go back to sleep, grumpy-pants."

"I wear no pants."

Xe tugged me as close as possible and I raised a brow as I felt xyr tentacles writhing against me.

"Oh."

"Oh is right," xe muttered sleepily.

"Maybe I should do something about that?"

Moss let out a very dramatic sigh, but I felt xem smile against my neck. "I'm going to bite you."

I squeaked as xe sank xyr fangs into my neck playfully. I laughed as xe released me and then moved me as xe rolled over, straddling me over xyr hips.

"You're so troublesome, little *tarax*. Waking me up in such a way."

I planted my hands on xyr chest and rocked against xem. "I'm trouble? You're the one who can't keep your hands to yourself."

"Because you're *mine*," xe growled, thrusting up.

Xe grabbed onto the fabric of the boxers I wore and ripped,

tearing them with ease. "Damn it," I gasped. "That's the fourth pair this month."

"I'll buy you more," Moss said, grabbing onto my hips and positioning me.

I moaned loudly as the tentacles thrust up inside of me, already slick and wet.

"Fuck," I rasped. "How long have you been hard?"

"Long enough that I almost woke you up with my tentacles fucking your ass."

"You should have—ah!"

I lost my words as xe started to fuck me, thrusting up and down. Pleasure shot through me, intensified by the mated bond we shared. I groaned as I took xem, riding them until the two of us were panting.

"Come," I gasped. "I'm about to come."

Moss grunted as xe continued. It was quick and hot and satisfying, especially as the two of us cried out together, our voices mingling as we both came.

Heat filled me as I shot cum across xyr abdomen, a soft moan leaving me as I melted.

Moss sighed happily, giving me a soft smile. I leaned forward, planting a kiss on xyr lips.

"Now, I'm awake," xe teased.

"You sure are," I laughed.

I stayed like that for a few more minutes, enjoying the feeling of being filled by xyr tentacles. Occasionally, I'd rock my hips again just because it felt so fucking good.

"Will you ever get tired of teasing me?" Moss asked.

"Never," I huffed.

Xe grinned. "I love you, little *tarax*."

"I love you too," I whispered.

Before I could slide off xem, xe reached up and grabbed hold of me, rolling us out of bed. I laughed as I wrapped my legs around xyr waist, holding on as xe carried me to our bathroom and to the large shower perfect for the two of us.

"Sex for breakfast," Moss said. "And then we can sleep until it's time to onboard."

"Yes," I said. "Sex for breakfast. And love for dinner?"

Moss laughed hard as xe flipped the shower on. "Sex for breakfast, love for dinner. What's for lunch?"

"Kink?"

The two of us stared at each other for a moment and then burst out laughing again.

I couldn't think of a better way to start the day.

Glossary

Cosmic Kiss:

SGT: standard galaxy time

Solartrees: faux trees that grow on space stations and inside ships

Hologram: a digital copy of a photo that syncs with all devices, from the company Hologram

Moon-jump: one week

Moon tours: 12 month cycle through the galaxies for the Galactic Gems

Zin's Planet Name: Lapis

Toras Planet Name: Tourmalin

Cosmic Crush:

Dhaarin: mate

Dhagonit: fuck

Rhan: idiot/moron/dumbass

Rhombo: desert planet in Cinnabar Galaxy

Cinnabar Galaxy: galaxy also known as the 'Wild West'

Cosmic Heat:

Augelite Galaxy: A galaxy made up of six planets.

Arbor: the Auguelite's largest planet. It is made up of massive trees and oasis', with beings that respect their surroundings.

Hörne Forests: A large forest on the Arbor planet

Crystal Oasis: A venue within the Hörne Forests

Sporev: Arborian word for 'sexual heat'

Tarax: a bright orange flower that blooms every few years in certain oases. It has a long stamen and an intoxicating scent.

Pollinai: lover

Pollinay: mate

Clio's Creatures

Hello Creatures!

My name is Clio Evans and I am so excited to introduce myself to you! I'm a lover of all things that go bump in the night, fancy peens, coffee, and chocolate.

IF you had the chance to be matched with a monster or alien— what kind would you choose?!

Let me know by joining me on FB and Instagram. I'm a sucker for werewolves (and swoony tentacle aliens) to this day.

Also by Clio Evans

Creature Cafe Series

Little Slice of Hell

Little Sip of Sin

Little Lick of Lust

Little Shock of Hate

Little Piece of Sass

Little Song of Pain

Little Taste of Need

Little Risk of Fall

Little Wings of Fate

Little Souls of Fire

Little Kiss of Snow: A Creature Cafe Christmas Anthology

Little Drop of Blood

Little Heart of Stone

Little Spark of Flame

Warts & Claws Inc. Series

Not So Kind Regards

Not So Best Wishes

Not So Thanks in Advance

Not So Yours Truly

Not So Much Appreciated

Freaks of Nature Duet

Doves & Demons

Demons & Doves

Three Fates Mafia Series

Thieves & Monsters

Killers & Monsters

Queens & Monsters

Kings & Monsters

Heroes & Monsters (coming 2025)

Villains & Monsters (coming 2025)

Galactic Gems Series

Cosmic Kiss

Cosmic Crush

Cosmic Heat

Small Town Romance by Clio

Broken Beginnings (Citrus Cove 1)

Stolen Chances (coming 2025)

Hidden Roots (coming 2025)

Standalone

Nocturnal (A Dark Academia Monster Romance)

Printed in Great Britain
by Amazon